Murder—
Queen High

MURDER—
Queen High

Bob WADE

Bill MILLER

WILDSIDE PRESS

Complete and Unabridged

God Save the Weasel
Pop Goes the Queen

...Spoonerism

CHAPTER ONE

ODELL WALKED hesitantly up the stairway toward the office. His right hand was plunged into the coat pocket of his brown suit. It clutched the crumpled yellow shape of a telegram.

The barrel of the .32 under his left arm still felt warm.

He halted before the oak-paneled door, teetering back and forth on small feet. Then he knocked. A man's bass voice rumbled, "Come in." Odell opened the door and stepped inside, the set of his plump shoulders defensive.

The office was big and leather-fitted, with a huge desk backed up against the plate-glass window that formed most of the east wall. Outside the window were the stucco buildings of Azure. In the distance, the Salton Sea mirrored the last of the afternoon's sunlight.

"I was wondering what had happened to you," the man behind the desk rumbled. He was dealing himself poker hands, feeding the cards deftly onto the desk top with meaty hands that had heavy lawns of black hair on their backs.

"Things come up, Mr. Barselou," Odell said and tried to keep nervousness from breaking out on his smooth fleshy face.

Barselou was massive, even behind the giant leather and brass stud desk. Careful grooming brought out his best points and played down the height and weight and boldness of feature that could have been frightening. His pale blue sports suit was tailored by the best man in Hollywood—a creative artist who was flown to Azure three times a year to outfit him. The forest of jet hair was kept carefully oiled and combed back into a smooth civilized cap with a neat stripe of scalp down the center. Barselou was shaved twice a day and pow-

1

dered to reduce the dark cloud that hung about his heavy jaw. But his mouth was pleasant and curved and his colorless eyes picked up the blue of his suit. Complemented by any other color, they were no warmer, no friendlier than nailheads.

These eyes transfixed Odell across the office. "Something's wrong. What's happened?"

Odell sighed and took his right hand out of his coat pocket. He slid the crumpled telegram across the desk to Barselou. The big man smoothed it flat and read it silently.

MEET ME LAS DUNAS HOTEL PRONTO PER ARRANGEMENT WON POT ON QUEEN HIGH STRAIGHT It was addressed to Mr. and Mrs. John Jones, General Delivery, San Diego.

There was no emotion on the stony face when he finished. "Let's have it."

"It's Anglin. It's the double cross."

"How do you know?"

"After he reported to you this morning, he went down to the telegraph office. I found that out by asking around. I didn't like that story of his, anyway. Sounded like a stall." Odell shrugged. "Well, that's the wire he sent. I used my deputy sheriff's badge to get a copy. And your name."

With one corded fist, Barselou wadded the paper slowly and dropped the yellow ball into the wastebasket beside the desk. "Then he's found the Queen—no matter what he said this morning."

"Looks that way."

"That's too bad. I liked Anglin all right." He asked softly, "Where you holding him?"

Odell shifted uncomfortably. "Well—"

"At my place?"

"I found him a couple hours ago. And I lost him."

Barselou stood up quickly. "Lost him? You let him get away from you?"

"He knew I was on his tail. It was up in one of those

2

canyons near the hotel. I tried to stop him. I shot at him but I—"

Barselou flattened both palms on the desk top and leaned his weight on them. "Odell, if you'd killed Anglin I'd have broken you in two. I'm not going to lose the Queen after all I've spent tracking her down. Understand?"

"I know, chief."

"You did good getting that telegram. But don't start thinking for yourself. That's not your job." Barselou turned and scowled out at the twilight view of Azure. He didn't have to look at it consciously; he knew it by heart. It was his town. It spread out before him like a map in perspective, sloping away to the east, rapidly at first and then more s'owly, till the grayish-brown desert blended into the deep blue of the imprisoned sea. Now the heavy shadows of the Santa Rosa Mountains were darkening the white, buff and lemon of Azure's uniformly pseudo-Spanish architecture. Barselou had prescribed the building regulations. Here and there the first neon signs of evening were coming to life.

Azure. California's Playground. The Winter Paradise.

He had picked his office site solicitously, anticipating what was to come, visualizing before its birth the town that now spread out like a gaudy carpet trailed carelessly from the Santa Rosa foothills. Only one site in Azure gave a better view to the looker and that was the Las Dunas Hotel, whose grounds began a block west on slightly higher terrain.

There were no letters on the outside of the oak-paneled door, but the people who mattered knew whose private office it was. Down the hill in the center of town was the business office, the Azure Development Company. Its assets included Azure's biggest movie theater, the only department store and a multitude of restaurants, bars and other tourist businesses.

Behind him, Odell stirred uneasily. "What's the next step?"

Barselou wheeled slowly to face him. His anger was gone

3

and his mind dissected the situation clinically. "Your job is to find Anglin. I mean alive. Obviously, Anglin has found the Queen and he's holding out. He's trying to sell her address to somebody else."

"Mr. and Mrs. Jones, huh?"

"I'm not going to be left whistling. So find Anglin, find him fast and find him first—before he gets to the Joneses, whoever they are."

"I'll bring him in—in one piece." Odell leaned confidently against a corner of the desk. He was padded enough not to feel it. Around town he was called "Little B"—about half the time that meant he was a smaller edition of Barselou. Actually, he bore little resemblance to his employer except in vague outline. But where Barselou was impressive, Odell was as unimposing as an erasure. He blended, and his round unlined face was easy to forget. Except his stoplight eyes set in fat like jelly-centered and unbaked doughnuts. His hair was light brown and thin. What he wore never mattered.

"Make sure you do."

"How about the Joneses?"

"Don't worry about that end." Barselou sat down and drew a scratch pad to him. With a heavy lead pencil he wrote MR. AND MRS. JONES in capital letters. "They don't know we've read Anglin's wire. A couple from San Diego checking into the Las Dunas this evening shouldn't be hard to spot."

Deliberately, he ran a thick black line through the words on the pad.

"Welcome to Azure, sir. And now if you'll please put your John Henry right here . . ." The thin desk man spun the registration card around with undertaker's fingers. Opposite him, he didn't observe that the chin of the stocky young man had eased forward stubbornly as he gripped the pen. The guest wrote, "Mr. and Mrs. John Henry." After a pause for effect, he added "Conover."

"Mr. and Mrs. Conover. San Diego." The desk man did observe this.

"That's right," said John Henry, disappointed. He'd waited years for a setup to his little joke and now it had succeeded like a brick football. "Our reservations were for this noon but we got tied up. I hope it doesn't matter?" His jaw had retreated to its usual conservative position.

John Henry was no taller than average, with shoulders that were inclined to stoop and a body that was inclined to fat if left alone. Wavy brown hair had begun to retreat along the high forehead. His eyes were mild brown and pleasant. Most of his appearance matched their easy-going, affable gaze. But his chin was strong and moved forward indomitably oftener than John Henry realized.

He was dressed all in brown—sport coat, slacks, loafer shoes, and an open-neck shirt which leaked dark wiry hair at his throat.

Gayner, the assistant manager of the Las Dunas, looked lovingly at the registration card. "Oh, not at all, Mr. Conover. The reservation made by the company was just for Saturday —not specific as to time."

"Had a flat tire," John Henry insisted. "Other side of Borego."

Gayner smiled sympathetically, professionally. He nosed through a register on his side of the desk, then noted a number on the card the young man had filled out. "Your bags, Mr. Conover?"

"They're in my car. I'll get them."

Gayner wouldn't think of it. Instead, he struck a chime hanging on the stucco wall behind him and drummed a finger obbligato on his polished counter until a boy in a maroon field marshal uniform had emerged from a junior jungle of potted palms.

"Vernon. Mr. Conover's baggage." Gayner flipped him the car keys.

5

"It's in the first row of your parking lot. '41 Chevy. Green sedan. Tudor," John Henry recounted, pursuing the taciturn bellboy toward the great glass doors in the hotel front. Vernon was a sliver of a youth, barely in his twenties, with a mourning freckled face and repulsed eyes.

"I'll be back as soon as I can," he said with a trace of a lisp. And, as he struggled through the heavy doors, "—if I can find it."

John Henry watched him make it through to the outdoors and then looked around for St. Clair. She was where he had left her, backed against one of the ornate adobe pillars of the main lobby, nodding her burnished red head engrossedly but wearing a fixed smile as she listened to the woman who held her in conversational captivity. His wife flashed him an appealing look, so John Henry sauntered over to the pair.

"Darling!" St. Clair said in a thank-God-you're-here tone. "I was beginning to wonder if we were in the wrong town. You took so long."

"Sorry, Sin," he said and nodded a smile to the other woman. She was past thirty and imperatively blonde. In places, her figure was beginning to get out of control. Her blue eyes hinted shrewdness; they were out of place in a face that didn't show much of anything one way or another.

"I'd like to present my husband—John Henry," Sin said. "This is Mrs.—oh, yes, Loomis."

"Miss Loomis," the blonde corrected heavily, almost manfully. "Thelma Loomis."

"How do you do, Miss Loomis."

"Just investigating your wife, Mr. Conover. I thought I recognized her. I'm with Fan Fare, Campbell Publications." She said it as if that settled that.

Sin explained carefully to John Henry, "That's a movie magazine, darling. Miss Loomis writes for it."

"Well," said Conover, his interest undisturbed. He read

6

Newsweek and looked at *Life*, generally the night before fresh copies came. But he added generously, "That's nice."

"Gossip stuff," Thelma Loomis said in a machine-gun voice. "Features on the stars—marriages, divorces, who's chasing who, their views on life, love and the atom bomb. How they use up leftovers. What they do in bed." Sin looked slightly embarrassed. Miss Loomis, it seemed, had made a mistake. "A natural one," she maintained, "considering how attractive your wife—did you call her Sin?—is."

"That's a nickname." Conover abandoned his covert looking for the bellboy and explained for the thousandth time. "Her name is really St. Clair." The British pronunciation made it Sinclair and usage made it Sin. Sin listened proudly, never minding hearing it all over again. The nickname fitted her—even in the simple beige traveling suit mussed by the San Diego-Azure ride.

The thick flow of hair to her shoulders was nearly the color of a cherry coke. The undulating cascade started by her sleek locks didn't stop there; the same curvy theme was reiterated by her slim body right down to her sandaled feet. Sin's face was piquant, but not so pretty as it was surprising. The red hair called for a pale skin frescoed with freckles, but it wasn't there. Her flesh was a clear and delicate light bronze hue that contrasted disquietingly with slanting green eyes. Her happy mouth kept Sin from being completely sirenish but she still added up to a picture of lighthearted deviltry.

"I have to be on the *qui vive* for any of the Hollywood clan," Thelma Loomis was saying brassily. The actors and actresses had a habit of slipping away without notifying their Boswells. "So I'm a lobby-haunter."

"You got the wrong people, Miss Loomis. All we did was win a quiz contest."

Miss Loomis looked blank and Sin began telling her all about it. She had been chosen as one of the contestants on

7

the Thursday night Be Bry-Ter Quiz Show in Hollywood. "The jackpot question was to identify a quotation—and I did."

"The darn thing had been building up since Bunker Hill," chuckled John Henry. "So here we are with a free vacation. Rags to riches."

"I can't believe it. I've never heard of anyone winning on the Be Bry-Ter Quiz Show. And I've listened to it for years." She started noting down facts in a little spiral notebook. "Do you use their tooth paste, Mrs. Conover?"

"For a Bry-Ter Smile?" Sin grinned. "I guess it's only right I use the stuff, smile or no smile."

"What was the quotation, by the way?" Thelma Loomis scribbled some things that looked like pidgin shorthand. Sin looked vacant and knitted her heavy eyebrows together in concentration. John Henry chuckled again—he always got a kick out of this.

"I can't remember," Sin said plaintively.

Thelma Loomis gave her a come-now sort of smirk and waited, pencil eager.

John Henry came to his wife's rescue. "She can't remember now. Honest, Miss Loomis. That's the way Sin's memory works."

Baggage clattered on the red-tiled floor behind them. Vernon panted gloomily, "I'll show you to your cottage now."

Sin was ready but the blonde writer was after her. "What does your husband mean about your memory, Mrs. Conover?"

"Oh, it isn't much." The redhead was getting annoyed by the woman's persistence. "A party trick mostly. I remember nearly everything I read, that's all."

John Henry seized her elbow and started his wife toward the glass doors which opened out of the west side of the shallow lobby. He put an end to the conversation with an over-the-shoulder, "But as soon as she's said it aloud—

8

then she forgets it. Sort of like emptying a vacuum cleaner. Glad to have met you, Miss Loomis."

Miss Loomis let them go.

Gayner tossed a key attached to a plastic arrowhead across to the diminutive bellboy. "Cottage 15, Vernon," he said in tones as thin as his body. Vernon scowled blackly on general principles and picked up the baggage. The Conovers followed him through the glass doors and down some steps into a grassed and shrubbed sunken patio, crisscrossed with flagstone paths.

Three pairs of eyes watched them depart.

Thelma Loomis closed her little notebook and put it back into the pocket of her yellow linen dress. A quick glance across the lobby and her blue eyes sharpened.

A man in an immaculate white suit was sitting militantly in one of the armchairs. He had been reading a newspaper, but now he watched Sin sway down the steps with interested gray eyes. His hawk face was deeply tanned and in vivid disparity to his silver shock of hair. A white sun helmet perched on the arm of his chair.

And behind his shiny mahogany counter, Gayner gazed after the Conovers until they had wound out of sight along the flagged path that disappeared behind the south wing of the Las Dunas. Only then did he bring his eyes back to his wood and glass cage to stare at the registration card where it lay before him.

Mr. and Mrs. John Henry Conover. San Diego.

He reached out a thin hand and picked up the desk telephone. He spoke politely to the operator, "Give me Mr. Barselou, please."

9

CHAPTER TWO

CRICKETS CHIRRUPED like traitors every place but where he stepped. Anglin stopped for a minute to listen, hoping the bugs would shut up. They didn't, but silence hung behind him like a curtain across the grass and palm trees in the rear of the Las Dunas. Far off, weirdly muted, the sound of the orchestra in the Oasis Room stole out into the surrounding foothills.

His boots were making too much noise on the flagstone path. Better take to the grass, though he was pretty sure he'd shaken them off for a little while, anyway. The wound in his shoulder had opened again. It burned with a steady flame and the blood trickled down over his hand. Odell had been smarter and faster than he looked.

It was dark here in the canyon back of the hotel—a graveyards of shadows because no breeze stirred. He was the only shadow that moved. It was a good thing the cottages were white stucco under their red tile roofs. They strung out in a straight row for him to count. He couldn't read the numbers because the moon hadn't shown up yet and he was afraid to use his flashlight.

The seventh cottage. Anglin got dizzy suddenly. He'd probably lost too much blood and then he was tired to start with. Tired and nervous. But his shadow marched along the wet velvet grass, past the regimented hedges and the Moorish type guest cottages, nearly all dark now. This was Saturday night. Most people were still at dinner.

"Nothing better go haywire," he growled. He wanted to get rid of the whole thing and clear out. The tenth cottage. It was dark, too. He veered over to the opposite side of the walk. Just four more to go and he could deliver the goods and vanish. Be good to rest for a long time.

10

The thirteenth cottage and the next one ought to— He froze as a bat fanned skittishly by his broad-brimmed hat. God, he was jumpy. But why shouldn't he be? It wasn't any piker stunt to play two hands in this game. Both Barselou and —but he knew where the Queen was holed up. That was all that had kept him alive today.

Ah, here it was. He stepped confidently up the flagstone walk to the blue wooden door. From inside came the murmur of voices and a little light seeped through the Venetian window blinds onto his dirty leather jacket. Anglin was a squat man with skin as weather-beaten as his clothes. He braced himself momentarily against the white stucco of the porch and shook his foggy head. His calloused hand left a smear of blood when he withdrew it.

The ornate door handle felt cold to his grip. He squeezed it and stepped into the small living room.

Darkness here. Some light fell in a lopsided rectangle from the open door to the bedroom. Beyond that somewhere, a man was singing in an untrained voice, "Beautiful dreamer, wake unto me . . ."

An invisible woman spoke from the bedroom. Her voice was startled into a squeak. "Who's that?"

His clumsy fingers found the night latch and twisted it home. The noise made the woman say again, frightened, "Who's that? Is somebody in there?"

She was as jumpy as he was. But whoever she was this trip she ought to be better trained than to yell like that. He told her in a low voice, "Shut up, for the luvva Mike."

She let out a gasp as he moved into the patch of light on the carpet. Anglin could see her now, standing still as a rock before the imitation ivory dressing table. Her face that watched him with wide green eyes in the mirror didn't have any more color than the table top. The brush she'd been punishing her red hair with dropped from her hand to bounce softly on the thick shag rug. The haze of dressing gown over lingerie didn't conceal her long tan legs much

11

and the sight of them made him forget the pain in his shoulder briefly, very briefly.

Well, he hadn't expected to know her. The big boy used different girls for different operations. This one was a looker like the rest. But why didn't she catch on? The big boy had funny ideas about the value of women in work like this.

"Get out," she whispered. "Get out or I'll scream."

"Quit it," he said, leaning wearily against the door jamb. "It's okay. Where is he? I got it for him."

"If you don't get out—right now—I'll call the police."

What was she talking about, anyway? "You're from 'Dago, ain't you?"

She nodded.

"Then it's okay. Now for the luvva Mike get him."

Her glance went for the white French phone beside the bed. Anglin put his hand in the pocket of his leather jacket, so when she looked back at him, he held the little black automatic carelessly in his horny palm.

"I don't know what you got in mind, sister. But I ain't got much time. I want to finish the job and get out."

Behind the closed bathroom door, the man began to sing again. "Beautiful dreamer, queen of my song . . ." Anglin looked at the woman and gestured with the gun.

"That him?"

"That's—my husband," she said dry-throated, her greenish eyes hypnotized by the weapon.

"Get him."

"What are you going to do?"

He felt dizzy again as the room swam around under his wide hatbrim. This should have been the easy part and instead—"Get out of my way," he husked thickly. He smelled her perfume as he brushed the woman aside and rapped the gun muzzle against the door panel.

"Okay, okay," said the singer inside and switched to, "I'se comin', though mah head is bending low. Ah hear those gentle voices callin'—"

12

Anglin couldn't wait that out, so he threw the bathroom door open and stood staring. The man inside gulped on a drawn out "old" and didn't sing any more. He was a young fellow, not too big but stocky, and his body was still damp from the shower and faintly pink from a vigorous toweling. He wore blue rayon shorts with an elastic waistband.

"What the heck!" finally said the man in shorts.

"Oh, Johnny, be careful," the girl quavered. "He might shoot us!"

Something was screwy here. The advance arrangements had been specific about the cottage number. The only unknown had been the when and he'd wired that this morning. He squinted his wind-burned face and did his best to think. It was generally a different girl, but the man should have been . . . Was this more of Barselou's bunch? He gave up trying to think.

"I'm sorry," he mumbled and began to back toward the living-room door. "Reckon I made a mistake."

The stocky young man moved forward as far as his wife's restraining arm. "What's this all about? What's the answer?"

"Never mind, son. I—"

"Wait a minute—that looks like blood—"

Anglin ran out of patience. "Whaddya expect me to bleed —milk?" he snarled.

The young fellow looked grim. "I don't like the looks—"

"Nobody does, son. My mistake. I'm sorry I scared you and your missus. If you got any bright ideas, let them stop here and now."

He groped in the dimness behind him and found the night latch, unbolted the door and opened it. The two were staring at him from the lighted bedroom. Anglin started to say something else but couldn't decide what there was to say, so he closed the door and stumbled off the porch onto the soundless grass.

The shadows were still as tombs and he was one of them again. The crickets ceased their ominous music at his coming. He didn't have any particular direction to go any more. What could he do now?

Mr. Trim hung up the bar telephone and came back to his booth. "That was my company long-distance," he apologized. "Business. I'd never be able to afford a place like this except on business."

"Oh, is that so?" Thelma Loomis commented. She really should ask the little bore what his business was, but she'd been asking questions all day and she was tired of it. The spell Mr. Trim had spent at the bar phone, she had put in watching Sagmon Robottom.

The man in the white suit sat morosely on one of the upholstered bar stools of the Palm Room and nursed his second Martini of the evening. His white sun helmet lay on the stool beside him. Robottom was a tall man and his athletic figure was almost painfully erect. Even his silver hair stood up like cropped and frosty grass. Thelma Loomis thought, he's too well-preserved to be true. She chuckled inwardly at that.

Robottom's hard gray eyes brightened in the mirror as a blonde youngster with upswept hair slowly cruised the length of the Palm Room behind him. His sun-browned skin pulled tightly over his distinguished features; apparently there was none to spare for wrinkles. But a faint frown worked somehow onto his patrician face as Robottom lowered his big head and began to play again with the stem of his Martini glass.

Was he waiting to meet somebody? Thelma Loomis wondered. She looked around at the roomful of people. The fashionably dressed clientele clashed with the more primitive setting of a palm grove. Exits were roughly outlined by pineapple-skinned tree trunks. The roof, the walls and the front of the bar were all woven of tough fronds. Three live palm trees grew painfully out of the center of the tile floor,

14

their drooping frills swaying listlessly in the breeze from concealed fans.

Thelma Loomis drooped a little, too, as she remembered her companion. She wished she could decently desert him, but he had bought her the Scotch and water. Then she saw Mr. Trim's watery brown eyes across the booth table, also welling curiosity and waiting.

"Oh, I'm sorry—I beg your pardon—what were you saying, Mr. Trim?"

"I was saying that you must have quite a fascinating job, Miss Loomis."

She elaborated. "It's all right."

"Of course, it wouldn't appeal to me, but lots of folks probably envy you the chance to mingle with movie people." Mr. Trim pulled an ivory toothpick from his inside coat pocket and manipulated it dexterously. The Hollywood woman sized him up again. Yes, same grisly teeth as the last time she'd looked—discolored, broken, uneven. He certainly wasn't much on the outside, either. Small, nearly bald, a pug nose that made her think of a doorknob on a tan prune —what was she doing talking to this character, anyway?

"I really should have stayed in Palm Springs this week end," she said. "I just had a hunch that someone important might pop up here."

"And they haven't?"

Miss Loomis snorted. "The usual bunch of creeps. The only interesting people here are that cute couple in Cottage 15—and, of course, Sagmon Robottom down the bar there."

Mr. Trim tracked her glance down to the man by the sun helmet. "Robottom? Isn't he—"

"Yes—the Prince Charming of archaeology. You probably read his book." Thelma Loomis was scornful. "He popularized archaeology—made it just like golf. Robottom's the All-American Boy grown up."

"He looks like a gay dashing fellow," said Mr. Trim just

15

as the archaeologist scowled darkly in their general direction. "Worried right now," Trim added hastily. "But what's so unusual about the couple in Cottage 15?"

The blonde writer explained grudgingly. "It seems the wife has a peculiar type memory. Remembers everything she's read until she says it, then it's gone for good. And that won them a quiz contest. You know the one, Bry-Ter Tooth Paste. They got a—"

Miss Loomis stared. Mr. Trim, forehead pleated, had sprung to his feet. Their drinks sloshed back and forth alarmingly. "Holy smoke!" said Trim. "Are they here already? Cottage 15, you said?"

From way below her eyebrows, she watched the wrinkled back of his black suit navigate swiftly around the palm trees toward an exit. Then she shrugged and went back to the business of studying Sagmon Robottom's perturbed face.

"It beats me what happened," John Henry said. "I was just singing a song—surely it wasn't that bad."

Sin still wore the filmy dressing gown she'd bought especially for this year's vacation. She faced the open closet challengingly, rapping at her teeth with a knuckle. "Johnny, which dress shall I wear tonight—the green or the gray?"

"The gray." John Henry frowned. Now he'd gone too far in reassuring his wife about the innocuousness of the gunman's visit. Sin didn't even think it worthwhile discussing. He wished he'd left her a little frightened. "That gun looked pretty real. Why'd he bust in here?"

"Wouldn't you rather I wore my green?"

"Huh-uh." John Henry bent over and started lacing his shoes. "What do you think, Sin?"

"I think I'll wear the green."

"No, I mean about the guy with the gun."

"Oh, him!" Sin was more interested in pursuing a wrinkle on the green dress. "I guess he just made a mistake, like he said." Now that all the inside lights and the porch light of

16

the cottage were blazing away and the windows were fastened and all doors locked, Sin wasn't afraid any more. Besides, it had all happened so fast and Johnny said forget it. "Why don't we forget it? I want dinner. You hungry?"

"Starved. Okay, honey, we'll forget it." John Henry straightened up and stamped his feet. After he found his soft white shirt, "What was that he said about a message?"

Sin chuckled throatily. "In the first place, dopey, we were going to drop it. In the second place, all the fellow said was that he had 'it' for you—or whoever he thought you were."

After a while, John Henry expressed all his thoughts. "H'm."

Sin had put on her nylons, straightening the seams carefully before the long dressing-table mirror. She was adjusting her garter belt when the rap came on the cottage door. John Henry was still pants-less. Clutching the dressing gown tight around her, Sin headed for the front door. Then she stopped and asked him, "What?"

"Nothing," he lied. John Henry had started to say, "Watch it!" but had given the whole thing up rather than make a fool of himself. "It's probably somebody from the hotel—the manager, maybe." Not that they'd reported their incident—both of them had voted against any fuss. But Conover wished somebody would show up with a notarized explanation.

He found he was holding the heavy glass ash tray from the bureau. Sheepishly, he put it back.

Sin finally managed to release the night latch and the door handle at the same time. Vernon, the freckled bellhop, stood somberly grasping an envelope in both hands.

"Evening," he lisped. "You sure got this place lit up."

From the bedroom, John Henry called, "Who is it?"

"It's all right," Sin told him. "Someone from the hotel, like you said." To Vernon: "Is something wrong?"

Vernon looked at the envelope moodily. "I guess not. Here." He thrust the envelope toward Sin. "I'm supposed to deliver these."

"What is it?"

Invitation."

John Henry came up, hastily buckling the belt on his gray gabardine slacks. "Invitation? Where we going, Vernon?"

The freckled youth was pained. "From the hotel. They're throwing a big costume brawl tomorrow night. Everybody gets invited."

"Oh, honey!" Sin's eyes sparkled. "It'll be fun! I love costume parties."

Vernon's expression signified disbelief. John Henry wanted to know what he had against costume parties.

"Can't see much use for them, Mr. Conover. This one you're supposed to come as what you'd most like to be. Now isn't that something?"

"It'll be fun," Sin said stoutly.

"Maybe," Vernon doubted. "But I'll give you odds. Now, if I were running this place . . ."

After he'd gone away with twenty-five cents, Sin repeated, mostly to herself, "It'll be fun." Her husband laughed and put his arms over her shoulders.

"Right." He pushed a kiss against the tip of her unpowdered nose. "I'll bet if Vernon shows up, he'll come as a wet blanket." He spun her around and spanked her dressing gown once affectionately. "Let's get us fed."

Sin vanished into the bedroom, peeling off the misty garment en route. Her voice floated back to him. "I'd most like to be a woman who's completely dressed."

"Barselou speaking."

"Odell."

"About time you checked in. What's the good word?"

"Isn't any, chief."

"Where'd you see Anglin last?"

"He was trying to crack the hotel from Andreas Street."

"Then keep that Las Dunas sewed up."

18

"We are, we are. Incidentally, our· Mr. and Mrs. Jones have checked in."

"Gayner told me that already. There was only one couple from San Diego today. Now listen, Odell—tonight may mean whether or not we ever see the Queen. Anglin's got to be found and found quick. Get me?"

"Sure, I got you."

"Above all, keep him in the open. If he contacts anybody at all—"

"I'll call you back."

"You tighten up your boys and check over here. There may be some other angles. And get this through your thick skull. This is one time when it's smart to keep up with the Joneses."

John Henry had a red knitted tie wound around his finger and the collar of his white shirt buttoned and the wings turned up around his neck. The knock sounded again.

"Oh, no!" Sin said firmly. "I'm not going this time. I intend to get my clothes on."

"All right, all right," Conover muttered to his tie and the front door. "I never saw anything like—" He let his voice trail off into unspoken bitter comparisons and went into the living room. He remembered the first visitor in time to open the door only a crack and say gruffly, "Yeah?"

It was a wizened little man in a black serge suit and his late fifties. He had a big smile on his face and his hand was outstretched. "Mr. Conover?"

"Uh-huh."

"Mr. Conover, my name is Trim. On behalf ,of the Bry-Ter Tooth-Paste Company may I welcome you—and Mrs. Conover—to Azure."

"Well, thanks," said John Henry uncertainly and opened the door the rest of the way. "Won't you come in, Mr. Trim?" The representative stepped in and stood blinking in the

19

living room. John Henry finally shook his hand and they eyed each other awkwardly. Conover could see no suspicious bulge under Trim's left armpit. Surreptitiously, he switched his gaze to the other armpit in case the man were left-handed. Trim squirmed.

"Who was it, honey?" Sin demanded from the bedroom. It broke the stern silence.

Mr. Trim cleared his throat. "Mrs. Conover—" He cast a questioning look at John Henry and the younger man nodded. "Mrs. Conover—I represent the Bry-Ter Tooth-Paste Company. For a Bry-Ter Future. You know."

"Oh, how thoughtful," Sin threw out to him but she didn't appear.

John Henry waited. The bedroom doorway stayed empty. Mr. Trim shuttled his glances between them. "Well—I've been commissioned by the Company to sort of look after you—you know, see if I can do anything to help—"

"Cigarette?" asked Conover.

"Uh—no. That's what I mean." Mr. Trim's bad teeth showed in a grin. "I should have offered you a cigarette. The Bry-Ter people want to make sure you enjoy your stay here. We want to be positive you have a good time and—uh—enjoy your stay here."

"Fine. We want to keep the Bry-Ter people happy." Pointedly, John Henry lifted his dark-blue sport coat from the back of a chair and slipped into it.

"I'm glad they gave you a cottage," Mr. Trim groped for conversational subjects. "Much nicer for a young couple, it seems to me. I'm sure that you'll—"

"Enjoy our stay here," the younger man finished.

"That's it! That's what I'm getting paid for, you know." No arrangements would be too titanic for the representative to handle. A ride up the Santa Rosa Mountains where the beach line of an ancient inland sea striped the slope like a traffic marker. A trip to the grove of thousand-year-old trees in Palm Valley, just two miles northwest. "Many of these

20

palms show traces of fire due to the Cahuilla Indian custom of burning the family tree upon the death of the family head. It's inspiring, Mr. Conover." Or perhaps a horseback ride in the opposite direction to see the Badlands . . .

Mr. Trim paused here, ready to go saddle the horses. "Are you staying here at the hotel, too, Mr. Trim?" was John Henry's question. The black-suited man blinked and nodded. "Then we'll know where to get in touch with you—if we have to."

"That's right!" Mr. Trim nodded his old head with its scant horseshoe of hair vigorously. "Please feel free to call on me." He massaged the door handle wistfully. "I'm always available—day or night." His laugh was forced. "Well—this is good night, Mr. and—uh—Mrs. Conover."

In the momentary silence, Sin said, "Johnny, what was he carrying on about, anyway?" She appeared in the doorway, tugging the green dress about her. "He's gone, hasn't he?"

"No," said John Henry.

"Oh," Sin turned fire-engine red and went back where she'd come from. John Henry and the tooth-paste representative went back to looking at each other. Surely, thought Conover, this fellow can read the longing for food in my eyes.

"Well—" Mr. Trim made his final attempt to carry the whole thing off on a gay plane. "Welcome to Azure."

He stepped out onto the brightly lit porch of the cottage. "Thank you," said his host. But the Bry-Ter agent wasn't gone yet. He peered at the cottage wall beside the doorway and turned back. "Say! That looks like blood!"

John Henry sighed, "It certainly does," and closed the blue door.

CHAPTER THREE

They went to the Ship of the Desert for dinner. Just a block east from the Las Dunas, it catered to the hotel's wealthy clientele, a set that could pay four dollars for steak without expecting stock in the restaurant.

With sincere heartiness, the Conovers ate at a candle-lit table near the bandstand where a small waterfall rippled over neon-illuminated rocks. To the left of the waterfall, contorted ironwork stairs led to a small balcony that ran across the north wall and commanded a view of the entire establishment. It was quite a view. An orange peel of a moon had just cleared the eastern horizon and it all seemed the special property of the Ship of the Desert rather than due to an enormous plate-glass wall. The amber light from outside threw faint shadows against the restaurant's walls, which were painted in blues and browns to simulate the sweep of the desert. Palm trees—Azure's trade-mark—supported the décor to carry out the illusion.

Atmosphere was rampant—even the waiters wore vivid Arab burnooses—but the management had underwritten the lushness with excellent cuisine, and not the least of their drawing cards was Duncan Hines' enthusiastic recommendation.

Sin pushed back her plate with a contented noise. "Now if I can just have some coffee—"

John Henry reconnoitered after their waiter and then craned his neck still farther. "Odd," he said softly.

"Um?"

"I thought for a minute I saw—him. Our friend with the gun."

Sin's laugh blanketed her exasperation but John Henry

22

looked defensive. All the more so since the suspect had turned out to be just another tourist, after all.

"That was the first time anybody ever drew a gun on me," he said, almost complainingly. The duties of assistant personnel manager of an aircraft parts factory didn't satisfy a deep-rooted urge for adventure which lurked behind his conservative manner. He had never been able to make Sin understand this trait completely. Now that he had tasted excitement, John Henry was reluctant to spit it out.

"Well, as a matter of record, the whole thing happened mainly to me," Sin pointed out.

"Uh-huh. But it was me he was talking about."

"I don't know why you don't go ahead and report it to the police then."

"That's right—take all the glamor out of it—tie it up with red—"

"Why not?" she grinned back. "If you're going to worry about it, I'd just as soon get it cleared up—then you'll forget it and enjoy our vacation."

"Sin—I don't think you have any lust for adventure. A mysterious stranger with a gun, a bloody handprint on our own front porch—"

"Oh, I wouldn't say that. Just because I don't think there's a mad doctor hiding under our table or—or—"

John Henry looked sideways quickly and hunched closer to his wife. "That's the strange thing, Sin," he murmured. "I've had a kind of a feeling that we're being watched." Her green eyes didn't change expression but he straightened and flushed, anyway. "All right, all right—I know it sounds funny."

The waiter, plump even in the loose burnoose, was at his elbow. Conover flinched and Sin asked sweetly, "You having dessert, dear?"

"No, I guess not." Dourly, John Henry ordered two coffees. "Black. And the check too, please."

After the waiter had hustled off, Sin regarded her hus-

23

band with gentle amusement. "I suppose you think our Arab's been spying on us, too."

"I wouldn't be surprised. He's been at my elbow all through the meal."

"You're just not used to good service, honey. People who eat here expect attention."

"Well, I still think something's going on behind our backs. Something big." Sin hoped to herself that the portly lady at the table behind Johnny couldn't hear him. "I wouldn't be surprised if somehow we haven't accidentally upset some criminal conspiracy." What exactly, John Henry wasn't sure —dope smuggling, illicit diamond buying . . .

"But doesn't that only happen in South Africa? I mean, don't you have to have diamonds first?"

He waved the objection off as irrelevant. "Just an example, Sin." He nodded and locked his fingers under his chin. "We do know this. It involves a transfer of something from someone to someone. Didn't the man say he had 'it' for me? And he looked like he might be a miner."

" 'It' could be anything."

"I'd like to meet that fellow again. Next time, you can bet your life I'll find out just what's going on."

Her elfin face reflected a hint of alarm. "Johnny, he has a gun."

John Henry shrugged casually, showing plainly that firearms held no terror for him. After all, he pointed out, he had seen plenty of guns during his three years in the army— though he neglected to add that as an air force personnel officer his knowledge of them was more academic than practical. Besides, there were always means of taking a gun away from an adversary. Or so the training films had indicated.

The rounded Arab-gowned waiter returned with coffee in the rough pottery jug that the Ship of the Desert affected. He poured quickly and skillfully, deposited a woven salver containing the bill on the table and journeyed back toward the mecca of the kitchen.

24

"I won't be surprised next time." John Henry stared balefully at his coffee. "Just let anybody make a suspicious move."

Sin sipped in some of the steaming black liquid. "Good coffee," she murmured. "But I still think your imagination's running away with you." She jumped and screamed, "Johnny!"

John Henry had knocked over his coffee cup. All around, chairs scraped and customers craned toward the commotion. Curious eyes saw a young man with a white face staring at the bill as it lay on the woven salver. The portly woman at the next table said half-audibly, "I felt the same way the first time I got the check here, too."

Sin reddened, semi-angry at being part of the floor show. She looked at the spreading brown stain. "Honey, you've certainly ruined their tablecloth—"

But her husband's white face was curiously triumphant. "There!" he whispered.

"What? I can't hear you."

"There, Sin—that ought to prove what I said. Look at that!"

His forefinger stabbed toward the salver. Sin indulgently looked at it, at the bill lying across it. Then she stared, awestruck.

It wasn't a bill, at all. It was just an ordinary playing card. The Queen of Diamonds. And across the queen's face someone had written in a bold hand: "Your deal."

The headwaiter, colorful in his Foreign Legion uniform, paused at the top of the staircase and waited for the Conovers to reach the balcony. Sin held tight to John Henry's arm. He could feel her trembling a little and when he looked at her, the greenish eyes were sober and slightly scared.

Behind them, down the twisted staircase, there dinned the renewed clatter of dishes as the Ship of the Desert continued business as usual. All four pieces of the orchestra had returned to their stand and were mutedly tuning up.

The headwaiter knocked on the oak-paneled door at the east end of the balcony. A man's bass grated, "Come in," and the Foreign Legionnaire opened the door to bow the Conovers into the office ahead of him.

It was all leather except for the spacious plate-glass window at the other end. A burly man stood there contemplating the glowing pattern of Azure, his light-blue suit contrasting with the brown walls and the moon-touched velvet outside. He wheeled and took his hands from his pockets as the headwaiter closed the door to shut out the multi-noises of the restaurant.

"This is the owner, Mr. Barselou," he said. "Mr. and Mrs. —ah—"

"Conover," John Henry filled in. Barselou inclined his bold head. The Legionnaire started a sentence but his employer shifted colorless eyes his way and the headwaiter subsided, bowed again to the Conovers and left, closing the door softly.

"Now, Mr. and Mrs. Conover," Barselou rumbled in a slow-freight voice, "suppose you sit down and tell me what seems to be the trouble."

Overwhelming as both the man and his huge desk were, Barselou didn't gain complete domination. Sin sank gratefully into the leathery embrace of a chair, but John Henry advanced belligerently to the older man. "This," he said, and flipped the pasteboard queen face up on the desk's surface.

Barselou lowered his big frame into his swivel chair and picked up the card with the tips of his fingers. After a moment of study, he smiled amiably at John Henry. He murmured, "'Insipid as the queen upon a card.'"

Sin replied automatically, "Aylmer's Field. Alfred, Lord Tennyson."

Barselou quirked an astonished eyebrow but John Henry didn't intend to explain about his wife's trick memory at this

26

moment. He said, "That's what goes on in your restaurant. That's why I insisted on seeing you."

"What and why?" Barselou chuckled. "I'm further in the dark than you are, Mr. Jones."

"Conover," Conover corrected.

The man behind the desk snapped his fingers. "Sorry. I've been thinking all evening about somebody named Jones. Tell me about the Queen."

"Start at the beginning, Johnny," Sin suggested immediately.

"Yes, do." Barselou's face was fierce even in geniality. "Right in my own establishment—like a mystery story, isn't it? I'm quite a mystery fan."

"Okay," said John Henry. He felt uncomfortable standing now while the other two sat, so he dropped abruptly into the padded chair by the desk. "Okay," he said again. "It was like this." John Henry told what it was like.

When he was done, Barselou rubbed a spadelike hand over his heavy jaw. He swung his flinty eyes from one to the other before he spoke. "Incredible."

"I suspected that waiter from the beginning," Conover said truculently.

Sin was more tactful. "We're getting tired of that sort of thing, Mr. Barselou."

Pale eyes sparked. "Why? Has something else like that happened?"

"Not exactly," said John Henry, silencing his wife with a husbandly glance. "My wife means we're tired from our trip, that's all."

"Yes, quite a drive from San Diego," agreed the restaurant owner, fiddling with the card again. "The queen symbol intrigues me—it might be the calling card of a wealthy woman. Yet you say it or this 'your deal' inscription has no significance for you." Insistence raised subtle spikes in his deep voice. Sin shook her dark-red locks.

27

"What are you going to do about the waiter responsible?" John Henry wanted to know.

"Get him up here," said Barselou decisively. "What'd he look like?"

That stopped Conover. How do you remember a waiter? "I think he was short and kind of fattish—"

"He had red eyes," added Sin.

Barselou said, "I know all the waiters who work here at the Ship—I should, since I see to my own hiring and firing. The simple fact, Mr. Conover, is that we have no such waiter."

"That's ridiculous." The young man shoved to his feet. "Don't tell me a stranger could walk in here, serve us our meal—and nobody would know the difference! How about the headwaiter? How about the cook?"

Barselou remained undisturbed, almost mocking. "I hate to think it's possible. But what else are you suggesting, Mr. Conover?" Before the other man could think of a specific accusation, "Why don't you come out on the balcony, both of you, and we can watch the staff at work?" He led the way, his nimble bulk dwarfing the slender St. Clair.

The late supper crowd had thinned out. The small orchestra drifted syrupily through a pit-a-pat chorus of "I'll See You in My Dreams." Barselou leaned big fists on the balcony railing, a roughly adzed palm trunk, and stared down. "See him now?"

The brown head and the red head swiveled slowly, surveying the shadowy pit below. Figures in flowing burnooses flitted like clumsy moths among the candle-lit tables. But after a moment, John Henry nudged his wife's middle. "See anything, Sin?"

"They're all too thin or too tall."

"I didn't expect he'd hang around. He did his job and made a getaway." He turned around to face Barselou's big smile.

28

"Perhaps it was a joke, Mr. Conover. Perhaps even a joke intended for somebody else. Some of these wealthy visitors have elaborate senses of humor. About all I can do is apologize profoundly—which I do—on behalf of the Ship of the Desert. And to pick up your check, of course."

Sin's hand was tugging at his sleeve but John Henry's stubborn chin jutted out. Barselou's bland assumptiveness annoyed him. "That's very nice," he said, "but if it's all the same to you I think we'll take a look around before we go."

When Barselou spoke his voice had changed but his words were still polite. "Naturally. I'm anxious to find out anything I can."

Odell lounged restlessly against the stucco wall of the restaurant about ten paces up the alley from Date Street and smoked his cigarette with short, nervous blasts. Wadded up under his left arm was an Arab burnoose.

The luminous dial of his wrist watch read 9:15 and he wondered if Barselou had gotten anything out of the young couple. They hadn't left yet, so maybe the deal had worked out. He believed in forcing the issue, and the queen right in their laps ought to start some fireworks. Behind Odell's vacuously cherubic countenance a constant flame of impatience sputtered. He prided himself—and his employer agreed dryly—that he was a man of action rather than of ideas. No use fooling around with these Conovers or Joneses or whatever their real names were. The girl wasn't a bad-looking head, at that. He let his mind roam sensuously.

A faint scuff of shoes against the pavement twirled him alertly around, head cocked. Somebody was coming down the alley from the other direction, the direction of Andreas Street. Odell strained his eyes through the dimness and cursed the buildings for being high enough to keep out the moonlight.

The man stumbled as if he too were having trouble with

the dark. Odell slid his hand to the cold butt of his .32 and brought it out of its lair next to his chest. He let his cigarette drop and squashed it underfoot.

The footsteps stopped. Odell held his breath and waited. A match rasped against boxside and the blackness thirty yards away was momentarily shattered as the stumbling man held the flame in front of him, peering.

A silent laugh rippled Odell's fat. Talk about luck! After all the trouble, here was Anglin walking right into the net. Okay, he wouldn't wriggle out this time. He put the gun muzzle on the dark blob and walked toward the other man.

Anglin froze. Then he hissed, uncertainly, "Who is it? Who's there?"

Odell kept walking toward him. "You know who it is, Anglin. Just don't make any funny moves and you'll be all right for a while. The chief says no obituaries."

"Odell!"

Anglin whirled, tottered and groped wildly for the door in the alley next to his hand. Odell dropped the bundled burnoose and jumped forward, pistol menacing. Inside, he was laughing again. The jerk was walking right into the Ship of the Desert. Walk into my parlor, said—wait a minute!

Was that the glint of moon on gun metal down at the alley's end?

Before Anglin could find the handle, the door abruptly swung open, letting a dammed-up flood of bluish-white light into the alley. It blinded the startled Odell, but he remembered not to pull the trigger.

Then he could see the groping figure outlined in the doorway. And beyond that squat silhouette, eyes wide and excited, was the amazed face of John Henry Conover.

John Henry thought the alley had exploded. He barely had time enough to recognize the prowler in the doorway when the man was driven violently against him, staggering him. Then he realized all the noise had been a gunshot.

30

Sin screamed and jumped forward to grab his coat. "Johnny, Johnny, are you all right? Johnny—"

"Okay, honey." Automatically, he held up the leather-jacketed body by its armpits. He couldn't see anything in the gloom. Dying away in the distance, he could hear the sound of footsteps, running.

Barselou brushed past him into the alley. John Henry felt a shudder go through the figure in his arms. Sin was sucking in her breath noisily and staring cloudily at the man.

"Isn't there something—he's hurt—"

Wetness had dyed a somber circle on the back of the leather jacket. The circle spread. The man twisted his head and sighted painfully up at him. He squinted his foggy eyes. They cleared momentarily and recognition showed there. A gasp was born in his throat. John Henry bent over him to catch the words.

"You already got it," the man choked. "Don't—" Tears flooded in agony and then the head lolled helplessly. John Henry straightened, frowning. His wife was frantically clearing pots and pans off a low wooden table, preparatory to using it as a bed for the wounded man.

"Sin," John Henry said quietly. "Never mind."

Another heavy pot clanged to the floor. Sin fastened blank eyes on him and Conover shook his head gently.

"Oh, Johnny—"

"Dead?" Barselou threw the brutal syllable from the doorway where he scanned the body narrowly.

"Think so—or close to it." Together, the two men eased the flaccid form to the linoleum under the fluorescent kitchen lights. John Henry suggested over his shoulder that Sin go out to the dining room, but she stood unmoving by the wooden table, hypnotized by the scene. Barselou's big hand rested lightly on the man's sunburned wrist. Then he got up, grunting. John Henry did the same and for the first time saw the silent spectators. The great kitchen was packed with white-shrouded cooks and helpers, robed waiters and,

31

crowding through the swinging doors, was the orchestra, one or two members holding their instruments protectively.

The headwaiter was as white as his Foreign Legion trousers. Barselou lashed at him. "Phone Lieutenant Lay, down at the police station. Get your people out on the floor. We're still open for business. Musicians, get that music going. Waiters, your place is with the customers. Come on, now—let's move!"

Under his impact, the becalmed Ship of the Desert creaked, stirred and got under way again. The waiters and musicians faded away and the cooks bobbed their round hats over stoves and assembly tables, with only occasional surreptitious glances at the dead man.

John Henry, his comforting arm around Sin's shoulders, had turned her away from the morbid view. "There, there, honey. Everything's all right now." Her eyes were less shocked but her tan face still picked up some of the green from her dress.

Barselou paced the narrow aisle between table and alley exit, his face uncivilized and angry. He pulled up by the Conovers and his voice was barely controlled thunder. "What do you know about this man?"

John Henry answered him slowly, trying to look surprised. "Nothing. I never saw him before in my life." He canceled Sin's astonished objections by squeezing her waist.

"He knew you."

"I wouldn't say that. He fell into my arms, that's all. He didn't know I was going to open the door."

Barselou's colorless eyes blazed at Conover's innocent expression. He moved his lips a couple of times and then said softly, "All right—you don't know him."

"Maybe it was a holdup that went wrong," John Henry suggested. "Too bad he didn't get a chance to talk."

Then Sin protested, "But, honey—he did say something to you!" and Conover's warning squeeze came too late.

32

Barselou hunched his wide shoulders forward and his face glowed. "So he said something to you!"

"Well," said John Henry, "he tried to say something, but he couldn't quite make it. Too bad, too—it might have cleared the whole thing up."

"A pity," agreed Barselou but none of the grim fervor left his expression. "It might have made things easier for everybody."

"Dead all right," Lieutenant Lay said and got up from beside the body. Barselou, the Conovers, the cooks behind their now-cool stoves and two tan-uniformed policemen waited for him to work a miracle.

The second in command of the Azure police department stood with his bowed legs apart and scowled at the wall. He was a lanky man in his middle thirties with a horse face and arms too long for his body. He needed a shave.

The scowl swung on John Henry. "Mr. Barselou seems to have the idea that you knew him." Conover shook his head and kept silent. Sin still leaned against him, but she wasn't about to be sick any more and her tilted eyes were sharply alive. "Doesn't matter," Lay rasped. "He's not hard to identify. Name's Anglin." He kept watching John Henry.

When the scowl began to fade, the young man thought it was safe to ask, "Who was he?"

"Oh, he hung around town a lot. Did lots of jobs. Been lots of different things. Prospected some." He glanced at the sand that had spilled on the immaculate floor from Anglin's clothes. "Was a guide once in a while. Used to deal faro over in Las Vegas—or so I heard."

"Lieutenant—" Barselou interposed from where he was fiddling with a meat grinder. "Maybe that has something to do with the murder. A man like that is bound to make enemies."

"Maybe. A grudge killing. Some bozo he's double-crossed

33

—or cheated at cards. Then again, Mr. Barselou—" Lay gave a macabre grin "—this killing's right up your alley."

Barselou didn't smile.

Sin said in a small voice, "Whoever it was, he was pretty persistent."

"I don't get you, Mrs. Conover."

"Well, he was shot in the shoulder too, wasn't he?"

"Doesn't mean anything. Most guys with guns can't shoot worth beans, anyway."

"What's Mr. Anglin been doing recently?" John Henry asked.

"Glad to have the visitors take an interest in our crimes," Lay muttered sarcastically. Then he considered. "Not sure that I know. I can't keep track of everybody in town. Characters keep blowing back and forth, especially in a glorified tourist camp like this. We didn't have any reason to keep tabs on Anglin—until now. He might have been prospecting. At least, he hasn't been in town very often lately." He knelt by the dead man again.

Barselou gave the meat grinder a whirl. "Just a suggestion, Lieutenant, but a careful search of his clothes—"

Lay, already rummaging through the dead man's pockets, didn't bother to look up and Barselou let his voice trail off. He eased forward to stand near the body watchfully. The black automatic, familiar to the Conovers, came out first, to be placed on the shiny linoleum. A dirty handkerchief, a small compass and a notebook, pocket-size and with all the pages blank, joined the gun on the floor. After a thorough search, the pile also included a few coins, a half-empty pack of cigarettes, a box of pocket matches and a wallet. The wallet contained a driver's license made out to Homer Anglin, nineteen dollars in currency, a Social Security card and nothing else.

Lay got up and rubbed his knees. Barselou bit his lip and tapped the police officer's shoulder, drawing him to one side.

34

Sin sighed. "Do you think we can go now?"

"Shouldn't be long now," her husband said offhand. He was trying to read lips across the kitchen.

"Why don't you ask the lieutenant if it's okay? I need some fresh air pretty bad."

Lieutenant Lay came ambling back. "Say, Conover, when you told your story why didn't you tell me that Anglin said something to you before he died?"

"He didn't."

"Barselou says—"

"John Henry's temper flared. "Barselou's got a lot of ideas. Why doesn't he have one about that waiter of his that started us on the whole thing?"

The police ambulance clanged outside in the alley, its siren dying to a groan. John Henry guessed the expression on Lay's ugly face was supposed to pass as a grin. At least, after the noise had died down, Lay said, "Oh, we all have ideas." And he let the Conovers go.

As they walked down the alley, John Henry said, "Whew!"

Sin slid her hand under his arm and agreed. "Was that the adventure you wanted with your dinner?"

"No," he admitted morosely. "I didn't want to see anybody get hurt. It never seems that bad in stories. When people in stories stumble into a murder, they always come up with a clue."

Sin moved closer to him and nodded silently.

"Darn!" said John Henry.

"What's the trouble, honey?"

"Tripped."

He kicked some soft trash aside and they walked on. Behind them, they could hear a loaded stretcher scrape into the ambulance.

The soft trash was an Arab burnoose. Lieutenant Lay didn't find it, either.

CHAPTER FOUR

They turned into the palm-guarded cement walk that wound up to the hotel's front entrance. A rainbow of flood-lights, carefully concealed in the shrubbery, bathed the area in carnival hues and threw grotesque shadows across their path.

A lizard scuttled suddenly away from their footsteps. Sin suppressed a shriek, doing her best not to let their unexpected Saturday night get her down.

John Henry pursed his mouth. "If we only had some idea what that Barselou is up to—"

"It's nothing that concerns us, Johnny. We don't know he's up to anything. I mean, it wasn't his fault that poor fellow got shot in his alley."

"Look at it this way, Sin. We get that funny queen card in his restaurant and it's delivered to us by a waiter in one of Barselou's costumes. We go up to his office, which is probably just what he wanted. As soon as we're there, you remark that we're tired from our trip and Barselou says it's a long drive from San Diego."

"Oh," said Sin softly.

"Right. How did he know we were from San Diego? We weren't carrying avocados or anything."

"Johnny, he's been checking up on us!"

"Sure, and why? We're just two more people."

"He must think we're somebody else."

John Henry nodded emphatically. "That's the connection. Barselou thinks we're somebody else. Anglin thought we were somebody else. And Anglin gets murdered at Barselou's back door. It ties up to me."

They started up the front steps of the Las Dunas and he

36

realized they were practically running. They slowed to a sedate, unworried pace and pushed through the glass doors.

The lobby was bright and quiet and deserted. There was a youth behind the registration desk who gave them an overdone smile and good evening as they hurried by.

"You have the key?" Sin asked.

John Henry felt its plastic arrowhead in his trousers pocket. "Uh-huh. Surprised?"

"After everything else, I sort of expected your pocket had been picked. Johnny, who *are* we?"

He could feel his wife relaxing and he grinned. "The Conovers, returning from a festive evening with the police."

The sunken patio was drenched in soft amber light. Scattered guests lounged at the metal tables under gaily-striped umbrellas. White-jacketed waiters, carrying drinks on silver trays, scurried to and fro. The amber light made the drinks seem twice as potent.

A wide cement veranda ran down the north side of the patio. More of the umbrella tables were here, and broad doorways opened into the Oasis Room. The even percussion of a dance orchestra floated out into the garden, over a current of laughter, the hum of conversation and the clink of ice in glasses. The dancers were shadow people, dimly seen from the patio.

The pasteboard queen and the bloodstained leather jacket had no place in this holiday setting.

Their path curved gradually up the canyon of cottages. Darkness sneaked in on the two of them again. Most of the cottages were still unlighted. A few porch lamps beamed down coldly, reflecting from the white stucco. Somewhere up on the nearest hill, a coyote howled.

"I'm glad you left our porch light on," Sin said suddenly.

"Always thinking ahead, that's—"

"What's wrong?"

"Nothing, honey." John Henry could have sworn that he turned the porch light off last thing before they left. But

37

there it was, clearly illuminating the black iron 15 on the white stucco. He glanced up and down the row of silent cottages. The canyon was devoid of life except for the Conovers and the crickets. Even the distant orchestra had taken an intermission. Then he laughed at his abrupt ideas of ambush and they stepped up onto the porch.

"What are you laughing at?"

He fumbled the key out of his pocket. "Nothing, Sin."

"Johnny! What are you laughing at?"

John Henry punched the key into the lock. Then he withdrew it and said, "I'm not laughing."

"Then why aren't you? You were."

He looked down at the lock. "I could swear I locked it when we . . ." He let his voice trail off as he tried the handle. It worked smoothly and the door swung away from them into the blackness of the cottage. "Guess I forgot that too," he said sheepishly and patted around for the light switch on the inside wall. The front room came into brilliant being.

Sin's scream was short and piercing. John Henry jumped and swore automatically. Sin was wrapped around his arm, pressing her body half behind him, her eyelashes fluttering in fright.

A girl was sitting in the big chair that faced the door. Her round eyes were ponds of friendly curiosity. Under them, softly prominent cheekbones slanted into a tiptilted nose. She was young, with a lily-smooth face and black hair swept up over small ears and an ivory-tinted neck. Trim legs were doubled up under her and one porcelain fist rubbed back and forth against her round slight chin.

"What the hell," said John Henry, "are you doing here?"

"Yes," said Sin definitely.

The girl didn't get up. She had a small sultry mouth that seemed about to laugh and squeal "Ooh!" at the same time. It curved a little more and said, "You're trying to scare me. Somebody told you I like to be scared."

38

The Conovers looked at each other. Nobody was making faces or anything. John Henry said, "Well, that doesn't answer much of my question, Miss—"

The girl kept smiling, half-veiling the bright eyes. Her voice came caressingly from way down in her throat. "I'm so glad you came to call. I need building up."

Sin said flatly, "We live here."

The girl answered, "I live here."

"That's not true."

The girl shook her sleek black head slowly.

"Now, look here," John Henry began, then stopped. He pushed around Sin to the porch and looked at the cottage number. Yes, it was 15, all right. His lips clamped in determined lines and he marched back into the house, shutting the door firmly behind him. "Now, look here," he began again.

"Tell her, Johnny." Sin nudged him. "Tell her that we're registered here."

"That's right. We're registered here, Miss—"

The girl stopped rubbing her chin. With the ball of her thumb, she polished at one long fingernail, and her face saddened. "I'm sorry this is all a mistake. It started out like such fun. I was registered for this cottage less than an hour ago. Mr. Gayner was quite definite about the number."

John Henry regarded her with grim disbelief. The brunette uncoiled her legs lazily and stretched, her open-toed sandals kicking playfully at the crease of his trousers. Sin whispered, "Johnny, don't just stand there!" John Henry took recourse in reason.

"Yes, I guess a mistake has been made, all right. They've accidentally put you into the wrong cottage. We've been living here ever since early this evening, Miss—" He rammed a fist into his palm. "I'll show you!"

This could be proved easily. He strode into the bedroom. Their clothes, which he had unpacked himself, were in the closet. That should convince the girl that she was in the

39

wrong place. The girl had unfolded her graceful body—she wore lounging pajamas of some dark fuzzy material—and followed him into the bedroom. Sin brought up the rear. "Now, take a look at this!" John Henry threw open the closet door.

"Do you think they suit me?" the girl asked him seriously.

Sin said, "Oh, honey . . ." John Henry got confused. The closet was stuffed with clothes, but they were the wrong clothes—slinky dresses, evening gowns, dressing gowns, everything feminine. Nothing was Sin's, much less her husband's.

The girl leaned near him, looking at the negligees, and he breathed in her musky perfume. She pulled out a hanger with a black robe which, except for collar and cuffs of jaguar fur, was completely transparent. She held it up and looked at John Henry through it with purple eyes frank enough to make him glance hastily at Sin. "I found this in Mexico City. Would you say it was too extreme? I can take awfully extreme things."

Confounded, John Henry backed up and sat down abruptly on the bed. "I can't understand it," he said heavily. "This is our cottage. I know it is."

"We were registered for this one. We dressed here. Johnny took a bath in that bathroom," Sin stated, pointing the way with a dramatic forefinger.

"So did I." John Henry wished the girl hadn't said it just like that. Then she smiled demurely at his wife. "You must have mistaken the number this evening. It's easy to do when you can't see in the dark."

Sin folded her arms. John Henry recognized the battle flags going up and he got off the bed. "I," she announced, "am going to stay right here. This is our cottage."

"Well, there's no use being unreasonable about it—any of us," John Henry interposed. "Obviously, somebody—" he glanced at the girl, who was holding the robe to her shoulders "—has made a big mistake. Suppose I get Mr. Gayner. He ought to be able to straighten the whole thing out in a jiffy."

"And we can have our cottage to ourselves," Sin added for her own satisfaction.

The girl put the jaguar-fur garment back in the closet. "Good. Bring Mr. Gayner down and we'll talk till bedtime."

"Well," John Henry said, "then I'll go get Mr. Gayner." He had to brush past the black-haired girl as he moved around the bed. The perfume was as heavy as before. "I'll be right back, Sin."

"Wait, Johnny!" Sin scampered after him into the living room. "I don't want to be left alone here."

"Okay."

"And if you think I'm going by myself, you're crazy."

"Okay." He took her hand.

The girl came in from the bedroom, clicking off the light. She straightened her lounging pajamas and coiled gracefully into her chair again. "I hope you'll all come back. And will you shut off the lights as you go?"

John Henry blinked. "Huh?"

"Shut off all the lights, please. Thanks." A flick of the switch and the room was pitch black. John Henry, looking back, imagined he could see her round eyes shining affectionately at him. "And shut the door, please, too—I like to sit alone in the dark."

"Sure," said John Henry hollowly. "Sure." He pulled the blue door shut after him and hurried Sin along the path toward the friendly brightness of the hotel.

"I wouldn't have had it happen for the world." Mr. Gayner was prostrated.

"Okay, I understand that," John Henry said. He stood behind his wife's chair, gripping the uprights. Sin sat there fidgeting angrily.

The assistant manager leaned his gaunt body back in his swivel chair and clasped his hands. He seemed about to suggest a choice of low-priced caskets. "Faye Jordan is," he

41

mourned, "a child of whim. Whim and wealth are an uncomfortable combination. Cottage 14 has been held open for a week, pending her arrival—she paid the rental all that time, of course. When she arrived this evening, I naturally moved her into Cottage 14—which she had specified in her telegram. A short time ago we discovered a mistake had been made in her telegram. Instead, she desired Cottage 15."

"Of all the silly things!" Sin exploded. "What difference does it make if it's one cabin or another. They're all the same, aren't they?"

Gayner shrugged. "Exactly the same, Mrs. Conover. Believe me, I emphasized that to Miss Jordan, but nothing would do but that she have Cottage 15. To make a long story short—"

"You moved our things out," John Henry said.

"Just next door," Gayner soothed. "You're now in Cottage 14. I realize and regret the embarrassment which this whole business has caused. I had expected to be on the desk when you returned. That way I could have prevented this unfortunate episode."

"Well, frankly," said Sin, "this isn't the sort of thing I'd expect at a hotel with the Las Dunas' reputation."

The hotel man sorrowfully scratched his long nose. "These things happen in any catering business, madam. We consider ourselves fortunate when one of the parties concerned is reasonable. I thank you for that. Of course, I did my best in your absence—I secured permission to move your baggage between the cottages."

John Henry swallowed with difficulty. "Permission! Who gave you permission?"

"Your representative here. The tooth-paste fellow. Mr. Trim."

John Henry stopped pacing around in Cottage 14 and plopped down on the bed beside Sin. "I know how you feel,

42

honey." She was lying across it, fully dressed, and he stroked her hair gently.

"I'd rather we planned our own evenings. When everything happens at once, I get confused. When I get confused, I get scared. What's so special about Cottage 15, anyway?"

"Beats me."

"That Jordan girl's crazy."

"Sure. Just don't worry, cutie." There were two light taps on the living-room door. "There's our boy now."

He was right. Mr. Trim stood blinking on the porch, brown eyes as limpid as ever. His small mouth and bald head reminded John Henry of an underfed Humpty Dumpty.

"Come in, Mr. Trim," Conover greeted him. "My wife wanted to see you."

The tooth-paste man sidled in apprehensively, turning his flat straw hat around and around with nervous fingers. He obeyed John Henry's injunction to sit and revolved the hat until Sin padded in from the bedroom, stocking-footed, when he sprang up again. "I hope you'll forgive this intrusion," Trim rattled in his high precise voice.

"We called you," clarified Sin. She folded her arms.

"I know," the little fellow confessed miserably, "you haven't been having a good time. That's why the Company sent me here. And I've failed." John Henry shifted his feet, hoping Mr. Trim wouldn't break down. "First of all, I'm awfully sorry the misunderstanding arose—"

"We are, too," said Sin, unswerving.

"Oh." This wasn't the answer Trim had expected, but he recovered. "I tried high and low to find you when Mr. Gayner came to me earlier with the problem. But you had gone somewhere."

"Thinking," the hardening John Henry put in, "that our personal property would be safe while we were gone."

"Mr. Gayner was so wrought up—I couldn't refuse—" The

43

wizened representative scrutinized the inside of his hat as if he had notes there. "It's my fault. I didn't realize a different cottage would actually make any difference to you. It must have been quite a shock to find your clothes gone and—"

"It was," John Henry said grimly. "But not so much of a shock as it was to find all our things had been searched."

Mr. Trim sat down abruptly. "Searched! You mean somebody actually tampered with your personal belongings?"

"Uh-huh."

"Oh, no!"

Sin said scornfully, "Oh, yes! We wouldn't say so otherwise."

"You see, Mr. Trim—whoever searched our stuff did it in a hurry. They didn't try to be neat. Everything's in a mess."

"I could kill them!" Sin jounced down on the davenport viciously. "They broke my bottle of peppermint. Now all my lingerie smells like chewing gum. I don't even think it'll wash out."

"I'm flabbergasted." Trim fanned himself with his straw hat. "I'm more than flabbergasted."

"Oh, well," said John Henry moodily. He couldn't keep angry long at a time. "It's not as if we were surprised. Nothing surprises us any more."

The tooth-paste representative stood up and said vigorously, "Something has to be done," and walked around the room in a little circle. Then he sat down again. "This can't to be allowed to happen in a civilized community. After all, I'm responsible, you see. For the peppermint and everything."

Sin fought against it, but she felt a trace of warmth for their unwanted aide. Maybe his bald head was solid rock, but he was sincerely trying to do his job. John Henry and she shouldn't take everything out on him.

"Johnny, maybe you should tell Mr. Trim the whole story."

Her husband's head came up in surprise. "You think we should?"

44

"He might have an idea."

"Well," doubted John Henrry. He regarded Trim's anxious expression narrowly. Then he attacked the story, wandering back and forth in front of the other man, trying to remember everything that mattered. The wounded prowler, the robed waiter, the playing card queen, Barselou's hostile attitude . . . Only when Conover got around to the shooting in the alley and Homer Anglin's dying message did Trim squirm and commence puckering his forehead confusedly.

"You can understand why we feel more than just ordinary annoyance, can't you?" Sin asked while her husband caught his breath.

Mr. Trim skinned colorless lips back over his discolored teeth and made clucking noises. "Say, I don't know what to say," he confessed.

"It'd make more sense if Anglin had given me something," John Henry said. "But he didn't. He just said, 'You already got it' and died. I didn't get anything. There's nothing in our luggage because we looked pretty carefully."

"Except my peppermint," Sin commented bitterly.

Trim reached over and laid his straw hat on the davenport beside Sin and folded his hands in his lap. "But somebody thinks Anglin gave you something, Mr. Conover," he said owlishly.

John Henry showed impatience. "We figured that."

"My point is that that is quite probably why Mr. Gayner was so willing to accommodate Miss Jordan. Moving your baggage would give him an excellent opportunity to search it."

"I don't get it," admitted Sin. "Why should Mr. Gayner want to go through our things?"

"Because he was told to, Mrs. Conover." Mr. Trim sat very straight and looked proud of himself. "You see, Mr. Gayner's boss—in fact, the boss of most things in Azure—is Mr. Barselou. Mr. Barselou owns this very hotel."

First, John Henry just grunted. Then he flung his arms

wide like a soap-box orator and said, "Well, how do you like that!"

Sin pounded one small fist against Mr. Barselou's davenport. "No wonder! But why?" Her tan face tied up in a knot of confusion. "Why?"

"Just more weight to your husband's belief that Mr. Barselou is hip-deep in this business, whatever it is. And there's no doubt that Mr. Barselou believes that you, in turn, are working against his interests." Trim asked gently, benevolently, "Mr. and Mrs. Conover—answer me truthfully. Are you?"

"For heaven's sake, no!" said Sin and crossed her heart. "All we want is to be left alone."

"Then," said Mr. Trim relievedly, "I suggest we go to the police."

"No!" The other two jumped at John Henry's outburst and he flushed. "I mean, no. Maybe now that Barselou's searched our stuff, he's convinced we haven't got what he's after. Besides, I'd feel like a dope telling all this extra stuff to that police lieutenant now."

"Mr. Lay didn't like us particularly at the time."

"I'd feel like a dope. I thought I was smart keeping some of this to myself—he'd give me life if I changed stories now."

The Bry-Ter representative got out his ivory toothpick and worked on his teeth while he considered. "Say, that's obstructing justice. But that's not my department. I can see why you wouldn't want to court trouble and I guess the police will find out this funny business by themselves." He held up his toothpick brightly. "We'll hire a private detective. The Company will—"

Now Sin objected. "Johnny and I have just been married three years. We still like to be alone together. It'd scare me to death if somebody was tramping around outside the cottage all night. We want a chance to relax and enjoy this vacation."

46

"No, thanks," added her husband. "We'll leave well enough alone."

"Well," said Trim disappointedly, tucking away his inspirational toothpick, "if you just want to forget it . . ."

A little while after that he retrieved his straw hat, took quite a while bidding both the Conovers good night and finally left. Sin and John Henry undressed in silence. The smell of peppermint essence pervaded the bedroom and kept all their reflections on one lurid track. A circular track that ended where it began.

"You know, Sin," John Henry mused as he buttoned his pajama top absently and gazed somewhere beyond the pink blossoms patterned into the wallpaper, "I was thinking about what you said earlier tonight. Who are we?"

She giggled. "Gee, we know, don't we?"

"We don't know who Barselou thinks we are. Sin, he's fighting somebody he's never seen—or he'd never have mistaken us for them."

Rolling back the sleeves of her robe contemplatively, Sin said, "But poor Anglin knew we were wrong—after he saw you. What was he trying to deliver?"

"That's over our heads." He folded back the bedcovers in a neat triangle on each side. "But first Anglin tries to drop off his 'it' here and no luck. Then he tries to give it to Barselou—and gets stopped."

"What did you do with my curlers?" Sin found them where she'd laid them on the ivory dresser. "Poor guy—trying so hard to peddle his something."

John Henry stuffed his handkerchief under his pillow, lit a cigarette and sprawled on the bed. "But here he's headed for Barselou—right at his back door—and bang! He gets delirious and thinks he's given something to me. Why me?"

"Maybe he thought you were Barselou," his wife said. "You've been putting on weight lately."

"No," said John Henry, pointedly ignoring her, "it was

47

probably a mistake. You know, he'd seen me in the cottage when he was looking for somebody else. When he was shot, his subconscious mind—"

"I had a philosophy prof at State that explained things like you do," said Sin, gathering up her equipment. "And I got a D."

Her husband chuckled. "Only because you were sexy-looking. You deserved an F. Anyway, mistake or not, Anglin decided to give it to me instead of Barselou."

"That'd be swell—except that you didn't get anything, you don't know what you didn't get and you don't know where it is now." She started for the bathroom. "We'll leave well enough alone. You were the guy who said that."

"Okay, okay. But I notice you've been thinking about it too."

Sin paused with one hand on the doorknob. "Suppose Anglin came up the canyon counting the cottages instead of reading the numbers. That's what I've been thinking."

"Suppose he did. It's dark and it'd be easier than walking up on every front porch."

"You know how some buildings and hotels don't have any thirteenth floor? 'Cause people are superstitious? So they just skip that number."

"Wait a minute—I see what you mean, Sin—"

"Uh-huh. I'll bet there's no Cottage 13."

"Sure, that's it! Clever girl, honey. That means if Anglin came along counting cottages—and got our old Cottage 15 —he was one number over."

"See, Johnny? Anglin came into the fourteenth cottage. But he wanted Cottage 14. Now let's drop it."

John Henry swung his legs off the bed and sat up excitedly. "Hey, maybe Anglin was going to meet the girl here in 14. Anglin makes a mistake and comes to 15, instead. As soon as she finds it out—wait a minute! How'd she find it out?"

Sin sighed. "Does it matter?"

48

"Sure. After Anglin left, you had me turn the porch light on, Sin. She could have seen the blood next to the door where he put his hand. So she guesses her man has been there and insists on having the cottage he visited. Make sense?"

"I guess so."

"She figures that Anglin left whatever he was to deliver in 15. So she wants to have the cottage and a good chance to look for it. Just in case, our stuff is searched, too."

"Well, which side do you have your Miss Jordan on?" Sin asked. "Did she spill the peppermint or did Barselou's Mr. Gayner? I'm lost." She opened the bathroom door.

"You know, Sin," said John Henry, pleasantly thoughtful, "I think it would be a smart thing if I tried to get chummy with the Jordan girl tomorrow and—"

Sin stopped right where she was. "Oh, you do!"

"Well, I just thought that she could probably clear things up for me in about two minutes. That's all."

"I don't doubt it. She looks like it, all right."

"You jealous?" John Henry asked in pleased tones.

"Well, maybe just a little bit."

"Don't be a dope. You don't have a thing to be jealous about and you know it."

"Oh, I don't know," said his wife grudgingly. "Maybe you like that slinky type."

"I like my women redheaded. With green eyes. And . . ." With both hands he traced a symmetrical outline in the air.

"Johnny, you're terrible." The click of the bathroom latch put a decisive end to the conversation.

"Hey, how long you going to be in there?"

CHAPTER FIVE

THE MORNING SUN sent golden rays like soft-tipped arrows, prodding the silent town to its feet, caressing the pale buildings, driving darkness slowly from the streets, invading the palm-shaded grounds of the hotel upon the hill.

Among the shadows of the chill morgue, the police surgeon stripped the sheet away from the slab and wrinkled his nose distastefully. In the tiny room next to his office, Lieutenant Lay sprawled on his back and snored. Barselou turned off his desk lamp as morning glow began to seep through the plate-glass window. He scowled again at the worn map on his desk and penciled a faint cross upon it. Odell slouched at the counter of the Tomahawk Drive-Inn, drinking his second cup of coffee of the day. Munching a piece of dry toast in the already-steaming kitchen of the Las Cunas, Vernon expected the worst: that some cottage would want room service. Upstairs, Sagmon Robottom commenced a short note to his wife, decided to do his setting-up exercises instead. The portable typewriter in Thelma Loomis' second floor room had been clattering for fifteen minutes. Gayner stood in the lobby and critically surveyed the tile floor, still needing its initial sweeping. Humming happily, Mr. Trim cleaned his teeth. In Cottage 15, Faye Jordan painted her toenails and waited for the phone to ring.

In Cottage 14, Sin pulled the covers tighter into her mussed red hair, dreaming she was being chased over foot-gripping sand dunes by a Queen of Diamonds. And John Henry Conover sneaked outdoors to see if there was a Cottage 13.

There was not.

Disconsolate, Vernon departed with the dirty dishes and

50

the few remnants of breakfast. Sin returned to the living room a moment later, her hair brushed into a smooth pageboy that glinted like a ruby.

"Johnny, what are you doing?"

John Henry stopped peeking outdoors between slats of the Venetian blinds and spun hastily, his round face guilty. "Just—looking out," was the best he could think of.

"What at?" Sin went to the window herself. "Oh!" She raised one stern eyebrow at her husband. The occupant of Cottage 15 was disappearing down the flagstone path toward the hotel. There was a great deal of pale skin which her white knitted bathing suit didn't cover.

"Just checking up," John Henry said lamely.

"Oh, yeah?"

"I heard her door slam and I was curious. Ever since you figured out that cottage number business—"

"Now see here, John Henry—"

John Henry sabotaged her objections. He seized her pliant body, bent it back across his arm, bit the tip of her nose gently and lifted her back to her feet. Sin came up laughing.

"What have you got in your pocket, anyway?" she wanted to know. Her hand plunged into the breast pocket of his dark-blue sport coat. "Oh," she said, "here's your pencil," and dropped the Eversharp back into his pocket. Sin pivoted happily away from him, her full peasant skirt whirling about her bare legs. "What a wonderful place to be!" Then she stopped. "Honey, what's the matter?"

John Henry's grin had vanished. He put a slow hand into his breast pocket and pulled the pencil into view again. His forehead had corrugated into puzzled lines. "Funny," he said.

"Johnny, is something wrong?"

He didn't raise his eyes from the Eversharp. "This isn't my pencil."

"You sure?"

"Of course I'm sure. Never saw it before in my life."

Sin laughed. "Well, I wouldn't worry about it. You probably picked it up somewhere by mistake. Probably when we registered."

He paid no attention. The pencil was an ordinary Eversharp, colored black and sea-green, with a gold point and a removable eraser. "That's what he meant."

"Who meant? What are you talking about?"

"Anglin. 'You already got it.' This is what I've got, Sin. Anglin stuck this in my pocket when he fell against me last night."

His wife sobered. The sunshine filtering through the Venetian blinds wasn't warm on her any more. "Let's throw it away, Johnny."

"No. Everything I said last night might be right. We should have guessed a pencil before. Remember? In his pockets, Anglin had something to write *on* but nothing to write *with*."

"Let's just throw it away. We came up here to have fun."

Ordinarily, John Henry would have given in to this typical wifely illogicality. But in his hand was Aladdin's lamp, Long John Silver's map, Ali Baba's magic phrase. Strange excitement gripped him and he temporized. "Well—let's just look at it a little first." Sin sighed and lost.

He turned the Eversharp over and over, while his brown eyes scrutinized its scratched surface. He gave an impatient grunt.

"What are you looking for, honey?"

John Henry took off the removable eraser and peered into the dark recesses of the cylinder. There seemed to be something wrapped tightly around the pencil's lead cartridge. He probed for it with a forefinger, then borrowed one of Sin's bobby pins. A couple of grunts later, he breathed out in satisfaction and pried a long narrow strip of tightly rolled paper from the interior of the pencil. "Well!" he announced happily.

52

"Quick, open it up! What is it?" Now the excitement had Sin too, and she crowded close against her husband's shoulder.

The paper was oiled and the tight rolling made it hard to handle since it kept coiling up between John Henry's fingers. The Conovers perused the column of writing on the paper strip and then looked at each other for an answer.

"What do you make out of that?" John Henry wanted to know.

"See?" Sin rejoined. Her point was that they didn't know any more now than they had before and they should have thrown the pencil away to begin with.

The writing on the paper resembled mostly an incredibly long safe combination. "Is that what it is?" John Henry asked.

"That long?"

"What else could it be?"

Sin thought for a moment. "Theater seats?" It was her husband's turn to laugh scornfully. She took the narrow strip of oiled paper from him and read it off slowly, carefully. "R-1. L-3. R-2. L-1. R-2. L-3. R-1. L-2. R-1. L-1. R-2. L-3. R-2. L-5. R-1. L-3. R-2. L-1. R-1."

"Must be a code," John Henry muttered. "R and L usually stand for right and left, but maybe this is a cipher."

"I don't know," Sin admitted. Then she added, "I don't want to know."

John Henry wound up the oiled paper and replaced it in the barrel of the Eversharp. This done, he began to amble around the room, speculatively appraising the walls and furniture.

"What are you up to now?"

"Sin, what's the most likely place to find a pencil?"

"I don't know—in the desk, I guess."

John Henry nodded. Sin could tell from the set of his mouth that his mind was made up about something. He pulled open the center drawer of the small redwood writing

53

desk, deposited the Eversharp reverently in the pencil trough, and closed the drawer again. "Psychology," he explained condescendingly. "The best place to hide anything is right under people's noses. They never think to look in the obvious places."

Sin remembered her own luck along this line in parlor games but said nothing. The sooner the pencil was stolen and gone, the better. "Hey, where you going, Johnny?"

"Back in a few minutes," John Henry said from the doorway. "After all that's happened, I want to grill this Jordan woman."

"Johnny, you come back here!"

"I won't be long—"

"John Henry—I warn you—"

"I know you'll be reasonable, Sin."

John Henry Conover closed the blue door in time to block the pillow hurled by his reasonable wife.

"Make it good," Barselou gritted between his teeth to the plate-glass window. "Or make it funny. I'd like to laugh."

Behind him, across the broad desk, Odell quailed in the leather chair and pounded a pudgy hand impotently against the armrest. "I didn't shoot him!"

"If you hadn't been in such a hurry with your gun last night, Anglin would have strolled right in here. We'd have a few right answers instead of a flock of wrong guesses."

"I knew you'd take it this way," muttered Odell miserably.

Barselou turned to consider him sarcastically. "You want a merit badge or something, fat boy? You not only kill off the goose but you make it so hot around here we can't even look for the eggs."

"I didn't kill him," the plump aide repeated wearily. "Maybe Conover did, I don't know."

"Sure—Conover's got long arms. Reached around and shot Anglin in the back. Then he swallowed the gun."

54

"They didn't have to come alone. Maybe they brought some armor along. I tell you I saw somebody pull a gun down at the end of the alley." Odell's eyes were redder than ever and his round cheeks twitched. "Lay can tell you—that's not my bullet in Anglin's back."

Barselou snorted. "Ask Lay—that's your best yet. We'd all be in the gas chamber. They don't call it anything but first degree when you plug a guy in the shoulder, chase him around all evening, then drill him through the back. And then this!" He yanked open a bottom drawer and lifted yards of gay cloth into view. It was the Arab burnoose. "You leave this lying in the alley. Didn't want to make Lay guess at anything, did you? Lucky I found it instead."

Odell wisely kept silent. After a moment while Barselou clenched and unclenched his big fists, he thought it safe to ask, "What do you want me to do now?"

"Nothing," Barselou snapped. "You're dead on this job. Get out to my place and lay low till this blows over."

"Okay." The plump man squinted in weary relief and heaved himself to his feet. "I'm bushed from staying in the car all night."

"Don't think I got any sleep, either. Odell, we got to find what Anglin knew about the Queen. She's too attractive to hide out forever."

"I'll wait for you to call me, chief," Odell said.

Barselou watched his henchman trudge for the door and scowled after him. Too bad Odell had canceled out his own usefulness. Good tough boy—if he just wasn't so quick on the trigger. But the Conovers would remember him. He wasn't good to have around.

Barselou's eyes pointed at the grain of the desk top, unfocused, analyzing. The Conovers. There had been nothing in their baggage, according to Gayner. Maybe it had been left in the first cottage—15. They'd been pretty upset about being moved.

55

That girl—Faye Jordan—was in there now, but he'd better tell Gayner to search the place carefully. No use overlooking any angles.

Barselou picked up the phone and began to dial.

"My business sense must have gotten the better of my social graces," apologized Mr. Trim. He put his straw hat back on his head and pulled it down tightly to keep as much sun from his scalp as possible.

Thelma Loomis sat at an umbrella-shaded table on the yellow tile bank of the swimming pool. She had been pretending to read the Sunday comic section while her eyes traveled a regular course between Dick Tracy and the silver-thatched Sagmon Robottom on the opposite bank.

"Perfectly all right," she said unenthusiastically. "You're not the first fellow to run from me." From the corner of her eye, the Hollywood woman saw Mr. Trim's gnarled hand close over the back of the other canvas chair at the table. Involuntarily, she groaned.

Trim said, "Thanks—I guess I will sit for a while."

Miss Loomis laid her funny paper on the metal table between them. Across the pool, Robottom idly kicked at blue water with his muscular legs while he talked gaily with a young girl in a white knit bathing suit.

The four of them were alone at the pool. Most of the hotel guests were Sunday morning sleepers. The Las Dunas swimming pool lay against the knee of a hill and had been expensively disguised as a small lake. A rough oval in shape, it was surrounded on three sides by the ubiquitous palm trees which were inset in the cement walk. Some of the fronds hung over the water. Like surrealist satires on the palms, gaudy beach umbrellas over round tables clustered along the banks of the pool.

Said Mr. Trim, "What are you watching him for?"

Thelma Loomis moved her gaze hastily. "Curious," she said. "I wanted to see how the old goat operated." Her com-

56

panion looked shocked. "He's got quite a reputation around L. A.," the writer explained gently. "Plus a wife."

Trim's "Ah!" could have meant anything. But he looked disapprovingly at the archaeologist and his brunette consort.

"That's no relic he's found there," chuckled Miss Loomis.

The girl's two-piece swim suit clung insistently to her rounded and enticing body. An inviting face crowned by braids of black hair was turned up attentively to Robottom. And he was putting his most charming foot forward. Even across the wide expanse of pool came the constant flash of blinding white teeth in the bronze aquiline face.

Then the silver-haired man got up lithely and fumbled in the pocket of his discarded beach robe.

"He's giving her something!" exclaimed Trim. "Say, is it —a key?"

"Not so loud, for Pete's sake," said Thelma Loomis. Robottom handed the girl a little card that looked like a claim check. She tucked it in the waist of her suit so that the edge showed against her bare stomach. Then he said something and they both laughed.

Mr. Trim clucked a couple of times. "A lottery. Maybe that ticket was a chance on something."

"You can say that again," the blonde writer murmured.

Apparently unaware of his audience, the archaeologist stood on the edge of the pool and stretched. Cords of muscle rippled above swim trucks that had been chosen to match his browned skin. The girl had cradled her chin in one hand and was watching him admiringly. Robottom said something over his shoulder to her. Then he launched his long body into a perfect dive, cleaving the blue water.

Thelma Loomis watched the graceful display he made through the shimmering water as he arched his torso and sounded to the depths of the pool.

"Say!" whispered Trim, tapping at her hand. "Another married man!"

Miss Loomis quit wondering about the card and brought her sharp gaze up to the girl opposite. The brunette wasn't appreciating Sagmon Robottom's performance at all. Instead, she had her pert face turned to a stocky young man in gray trousers and blue sport coat who had strode purposefully from the direction of the guest cottages.

"That's young Conover," hissed Mr. Trim.

"Of course," said Thelma Loomis exasperatedly.

The girl patted the yellow tiles beside her and Conover sat down awkwardly, folding his legs beneath him.

Robottom surfaced and blew out water. He looked for applause from the girl. Then he saw the man with whom she was engaged in fascinated conversation. The expression on his face was impossible to catalogue.

John Henry had no more than determined how to pursue his course of clever questioning when Miss Jordan said matter-of-factly, "I suppose you're here to find out how I got your cottage."

"Uh—well—no," he managed.

"Oh, sure you are," Miss Jordan told him confidently. "Your wife probably sent you."

"That's not true. In fact, she—"

The girl's round eyes brightened still more and she leaned a smooth shoulder closer to him. "Why, Mr. Conover!" her voice caressed his ear. Conover's stomach tingled. He felt as if he could warm his hands at her purple eyes.

He glanced around hurriedly. Sin wasn't in sight. A muscular middle-aged man was flailing up and down the pool, apparently disgruntled over something. And at a table on the other side, Mr. Trim and the fan magazine writer had developed sudden interest in the Sunday comic section.

"Now, Miss Jordan—" John Henry edged away from the white knit hip.

"Call me Faye."

"Now, Miss Faye—"

58

"Faye! With an 'e' like in 'easy.'"

"Now, Faye, with—"

"You're improving—Johnny."

"Now—" said John Henry and forgot what it was. The girl had slid along the yellow tile so that her bare knee nudged his leg. He couldn't retreat any farther without falling into the pool or actually getting up.

John Henry started to give the whole thing up when he saw the card tucked into the waistband of her swim suit. Too large for a calling card, it evidently had some engraved letters on the side that was against her flesh. At least, the engraving had dented through onto the blank side in places. What was she doing carrying the card around in her bathing suit?

"Let's talk," he suggested, torn between retreat and curiosity.

"Intimately," Faye amended. "You start."

"No—let's talk about you."

"All right. Do you know why I think you're cute?"

"No—"

"It's because you give a virile impression, as though you could—"

"I mean—no, let's you tell me about yourself." The fingers with which John Henry intended to steal the card from between her bathing suit and her stomach were turning hot and cold alternately. He fiddled casually with a belt loop on his trousers, wishing his hand wouldn't perspire so.

Faye put her crimson lower lip out. "Oh, you didn't want to see me at all! You're just trying to pump me, squeeze me dry and throw me away. If you don't build me up, I'll go talk to that cute boy in the pool."

She turned her head toward the white-haired swimmer for a second and John Henry saw his chance. He streaked his hand for the mysterious card. And she turned back.

"Oh, don't!" he murmured desperately and dropped his hand. Faye stopped pouting and her small full mouth curved into a wise smile. "I wouldn't think of it now," she giggled.

John Henry had dropped his unsuccessful hand on something warm and firm; he suddenly realized it was her bare leg. He drew back his fingers as from a hot iron. Faye put her face up close and whispered, "Are you a policeman?"

He didn't see any connection immediately. "Is that the way—"

"I'll bet you think I had something to do with the murder."

"What murder?" He had her now. John Henry breathed deeply, trying to discern the odor of spilled peppermint. All he smelled was overpowering jasmine which made him sneeze.

"You know what murder, Johnny. It was in the paper this morning."

"Oh." He'd forgotten about the newspapers.

"Do you think I did?"

"Well, did you?"

Faye Jordan shook her black braids disconsolately. "I wish I had. Nobody ever thinks I'm criminal. It's not exciting. Nothing's exciting." Her eyes strayed down to the end of the pool where the athletic man was resting, his brown arms flattened across the tile, the bulk of his body still submerged.

John Henry considered the engraved card again and was baffled. It had slipped down inside her white knit trunks. He said suddenly, "Why did you insist on changing cottages with us, Faye?"

Her wide-eyed stare was innocent. Conover sought in vain for deception behind the purple eyes. "I didn't, Johnny."

John Henry pounced. "Mr. Gayner said you did."

Faye rubbed the back of her fist against her chin reproachfully. "You don't trust me." Her generous lip trembled.

"Sure, I trust you, Faye. We—no, I just wondered—and then Gayner said—"

"Johnny," she crooned throatily, "I don't care what cottage I have. I can sleep anywhere. But that Mr. Gayner insisted that I move to Cottage 15."

"Oh-ho!" John Henry said. He heard a sniff from the direction of her turned-up nose, so he patted her shoulder paternally. "That's okay. I believe you, Faye."

She sniffed more happily and stretched her figure toward him as if she expected to be stroked. Her hand rubbed her hip about where John Henry estimated the card had slipped to. "I'm impressed," Faye whispered. "I'll bet we'll be as close as friends can get—darling."

John Henry gulped.

Sin clenched her fists hard. She said to herself: now look here, St. Clair, you are not—positively not—going to lose your temper. Across the pool, Miss Jordan was smiling sleepily up at John Henry's attentive face. Sin closed her eyes tight and gritted her teeth. Now look here, she began again.

But she was on fire, from the dark red page-boy down to the crimson toenails that peeked out of her suede sandals. I don't look so bad, either, she thought. In fact, I look darn good. She was wearing the filmy white blouse that her husband liked—"you know, Sin, one of the ones you can see through"—and the full peasant skirt. The ensemble chopped at least five years off her age and made her look a saucy eighteen again. Anyway, not like a cast-aside wife of three year's standing.

She speared another angry glance at the couple across the pool. John Henry was helping the Jordan girl to her feet. Her husband flashed a guilty look at Sin and then the brunette seized his hand gaily and started to drag him along the flagged path toward the guest cottages. Sin's lips pressed out flat in a thin red line and she clenched her fists.

The reluctant Conover was pulled out of sight between screening palms. A few paces away, Thelma Loomis and Mr. Trim were nodding and talking—probably about John Henry. Sin flushed at the thought.

Two brawny hands appeared on the tile bank at her feet. Sin moved out of the way to let the swimmer hoist himself

61

from the pool. She kept going, her mind made up. Fists still clenched, Sin marched determinedly after her husband.

On the other side of the palm trees, she felt the grip on her elbow, a cold wet hand. Sin shied away, startled.

A toneless voice said, "We had better have a talk."

Towering over her was the swimmer who had climbed from the pool at her feet. His short hair stood up in wet silver barbs. Water still trickled down his lean hard face and over the wiry muscles of his darkly tanned body. Only the girdle of muscle around the waist was beginning to soften into middle-aged heaviness.

"Well, I'm sorry," Sin said. Annoyance began to weave into her surprise. "I have to catch my husband before he—"

Iron fingers tightened on her elbow. "Talk first," the man said flatly. "One short warning before it's too late." His voice didn't match the vibrancy, the keen aliveness of the rest of him. The words came from between his white even teeth with scholarly precision. But his factual intonation made them colorless words, dead words.

The damp hand urged her off the main path onto a shady graveled way. "Who are you?" said Sin faintly. Jealousy of the seductive Faye Jordan had vanished. The cold tight band on her elbow spread by implication to the rest of her body.

"A person who permits no interference," was the man's answer. "I'll make you see the reason of that." Sin found herself trotting to keep up with his long strides. They were headed for a huge brick and screen building that loomed through the tropical foliage. She thought of screaming just as he stopped.

"Call for all the help you like," the white-haired man intoned. "No one will notice another noise from this direction." He folded his arms and his hawklike mask was intent, fierce.

They stood before the building. Its four corner pillars were bare adobe bricks. The rest was wire mesh that curved up until it seemed to melt into the bright sky.

62

Inside the aviary, hordes of bright-winged birds darted and soared in whirlwinds of color, enraged at the disturbing visitors. They flapped and cawed and screamed piercingly, flooding the air with outcry. It was inhuman noise, full of jungle menace.

"Pretend to watch the birds." The flat voice pushed the command into Sin's consciousness. He had released her elbow so Sin leaned weakly against the heavy wire screen. A white shape appeared by her head and long claws on wrinkled pink fingers reached through the mesh.

Sin jumped back, face gray. Her captor laughed and the sound was as toneless as his words. He slapped a big hand against the screen and the cockatoo glided away with a raucous screech.

"He merely wanted to be fed," said the man. "Inside that cage, the birds are confined in a shrunken world. They can't get away from one another. They constantly struggle for survival. The strongest win—at any price."

Rich-blossomed trees pressed in from every side. Sunlight through the leaves cast an odd pattern of black and gold over the dripping half-naked man. The din was tremendous. Sin bowed her head and put her hands over her ears. "Let me go," she begged.

Stronger hands pulled them away again. "Listen to me. My name is Sagmon Robottom."

The name didn't mean anything to her. "Let me go," Sin said again. Shaking her head didn't lessen the clamor in her ears.

"My business permits me no respect for feelings," Robottom said. "I get what I seek. I've robbed graves and rifled tombs to do my duty—immortalize the dead. I want you to recognize how strongly I feel about this entire affair."

Within the aviary, a new voice rasped. "Time's up! Time's up!"

Sin whirled. A black-and-white bird like a large and ugly

crow was sitting in a swing. It cocked its head at her. A flock of green and blood-red parakeets whirled by, making her vision swim.

"—not going to hurt you," the toneless voice was saying.

"We haven't done anything," Sin said, trying to understand, trying to make the man before her understand. "Why should we be—"

Robottom cut her off with a savage gesture. "Neither you nor your husband will be hurt," he said. Then he added, "If."

The black-and-white bird shrieked, "Goodbye! Goodbye! Time's up!"

"If what?" Sin quavered.

"If you forget all about this Jones business and go home where you belong."

Sin backed away, trying to remember who else had mentioned Jones recently. Robottom's long arm came out, shedding droplets of water. His hand closed over her shoulder.

"You're hurting me," Sin protested.

The lean bronzed face came closer. "I'm doing you a service, Mrs. Conover. This race is for the strong. The winner will be strong. Follow that reasoning through and you'll see you have no chance of winning. Stay out of this, Mrs. Conover."

"Goodbye! Time's up!" the bird rasped again and made a whirring sound.

Robottom took his hand away. "Apply that logic," he ordered. "No more Joneses. No more Conovers in Azure. Can I depend upon you to take that message to your husband? Stay away from here and stay away from things which aren't your business. Briefly, Mrs. Conover—stay away from *her!*"

Sin nodded automatically, blindly obeying the hard gray eyes. She started to say, "Who is—"

Feet crunched in the shady gravel path behind them. Robottom stepped to where he could get a clear view. He left a muddy spot where he had been standing.

He turned back to the aviary, a new mask of dignity

replacing the menace. Sin caught a glimpse of Thelma Loomis and Mr. Trim strolling toward the giant cage.

"That is an astonishing specimen," said Robottom and his voice seemed better suited for a lecture. "The Indian hill macaw. His vocal prowess—"

Sin left him, slipping down the nearest tunnel between the trees. The leaf-filtered sunlight, the half-human screams of the birds, the suave threatening of the trunk-clad man, had created a cold unreasoning well of fear. For that brief time, their solitude had been the jungle of another age. She had to get out into the open sun and find John Henry and leave this horrible place.

Somewhere behind her, the macaw screeched, "Time's up! Goodbye!"

It wasn't until she reached the sunken patio that she realized she was running as if pursued by demons.

CHAPTER SIX

THE ROAD was bumpy even in her convertible Mercury. John Henry conned the girl's profile against the speeding desert. Almost classic, if you liked a nose that regally turned up a little. Then he reached the conclusion that her chin curved toward the delicate throat too soon. It didn't balance the forehead which arced up to her ebony braids. Faye ruined his analysis with a boudoir smile.

"We're almost there now, Johnny."

"Good. Where?" She lowered her lashes enigmatically. John Henry couldn't get an answer for that particular question. Back at the pool, Faye had suddenly told him he would be interested in seeing a fascinating place—a secret place. Curious, but inwardly hesitant, he had allowed himself to be carried away from the Las Dunas, through Azure and out across the rolling plains to the south. A mile or so back, Faye had wheeled the Mercury off on a dirt road, still holding to a speed that made the conservative John Henry shudder.

The sun was midway to the meridian. Already the day promised to be hot. Heat waves were beginning to shimmer up from the mesquite and sagebrush-matted hillocks, dotted with yucca and an occasional tamarack tree. The road, though twisting and turning, hugged the Santa Rosa foothills.

Faye had changed her bathing suit for a play dress, pink with a faint horizontal white stripe, full skirt, low-backed and with a bare midriff. The exposed stomach bothered John Henry some; it always did in a street length dress.

What bothered him more was the card. He could see the

66

white edge of its stiff cardboard protruding from the skirt pocket on her left thigh. Why did she carry it in everything she wore? But he wasn't going to try for it again—not right away. It was all John Henry could do to stay on his own side of the car, the gay way she took the hairpin curves.

"Why don't you slow down a little," he suggested tentatively.

"Don't you like going fast?"

"What's the big hurry?"

"What's life? What's death?" Faye asked rhetorically, her eyes immense. "They answer themselves—*what?* The hurry is a matter of life and death. You have to keep ahead of time for excitement. Don't you ever read books?"

"I guess I haven't been getting enough out of them."

The Mercury leaped ahead faster than ever and Faye laughed exultingly. John Henry hunched down in the red-leather seat. Sin had been right. He should have taken her advice. It would be tough on her when she heard.

J. H. CONOVER DIES
IN DESERT CRACK-UP

He hoped they'd have sense enough to break it to Sin gently.

"There it is," Faye announced happily and John Henry realized he had his eyes shut. He opened them now.

The Mercury had topped a slight rise in the desert and was rolling headlong down the incline on the other side toward a barbed-wire fence which vaulted the road in the form of a log archway. The swinging sign spelled out Bar C Ranch in twigs. Beyond the fence, man's dissatisfied hand showed. The mesquite, sagebrush and greasewood had been banished. In their place sprouted feathery green tamarisk trees, rows of pink and white oleanders and, of course, the omnipresent palms. An attempt to maintain grass had met with only mixed success.

67

A hundred yards back from the archway rested the bulk of the large house. It was low and rambling, devoted more to length and breadth than to height. Wings sprang forth haphazardly to the right and the left. Much of the frontage was taken up by a long porch, shaded by a continuation of the shingled, slightly sloping roof. The ranch house was evidently constructed of adobe, plastered with a beige stucco. It had been deliberately aged in spots by allowing the adobe bricks to peep through. The pseudo-western air had been carried through with heavy beams which supported the roof and with wooden shutters on the windows. But behind these shutters, John Henry could see shiny metal Venetian blinds.

"Isn't it darling!" Faye breathed as she forced the Mercury to a jarring stop. "Oh, I guess I'm supposed to park over there." The car lunged forward again, pursuing the circular gravel driveway to a small parking lot. The lot was already occupied by a silent herd of automobiles.

When they made their last vibrating halt, John Henry clamped a decisive hand on the girl's wrist. "Now, before we go any farther—"

"Now you're talking!" purred Faye. She got up on her hands and knees on the seat cushions and thrust out her face toward him.

John Henry sank behind a determined shoulder and said, "None of that. Just what is this place and what are we doing here? What's so secret about a dude ranch?"

"You're so pent-up," she sighed and reached across him to open his door. Then she crawled over his lap and slid to the ground. "It's no dude ranch," she added.

Dubiously, Conover followed her. Faye Jordan had the mysterious card palmed in one hand now.

Within the semicircle of the driveway, a lavish flower bed had been established and rust-gold poppies spelled out the name of the ranch in capital letters. As they crunched through the gravel to the big front door, John Henry noticed

that bridles and branding irons hung from the huge support-
ing timbers of the porch. A weathered broken wagon wheel
leaned theatrically against the low cement and tile porch. Off
to one side, a hitching rail now tethered, not horses, but a
gleaming chrome-plated racing bicycle. Faye banged at the
door with the heavy brass knocker.

"Are they expecting you?" Conover asked.

"That's no fun." The latch rattled and the door swung
open smoothly, revealing dim cool reaches beyond. A battered face peered at them from the gloom. Crushed lips
grated, "Won't you come in?"

Faye stepped blithely forward and John Henry followed.
He squinted in the reception hall, his eyes accustoming
themselves to the murkiness. The man who had opened the
door teetered on squeaky patent leather shoes. He was
dressed in a black double-breasted suit with a black bow tie.
There was a lot of him. John Henry's reaction was: what a
well-groomed ape.

"Are we late?" Faye asked him, admiring his barrel chest.

The man bowed his square head and said, "Never." John
Henry realized he was either butler, bouncer or guard. Possibly all three. "Your card, madame?"

Faye flipped her fingers and the husky man caught the
card deftly. John Henry had his chance to see it—and he was
disappointed. The drop of his stomach let him know his self-
appointed investigation had been based on pretty flimsy
grounds.

For the card bore no queen symbol. Whorls and lines of
patterned engraving followed the edge like those on a bond
or a bank note. In the center was simply a straight black line
followed by a large C.

"Certainly," the butler said rustily. "You will forgive these
precautions—" his pin-point eyes cased the pair "—but they
have been found to be necessary. My name is Sidney, madame."

"I'm Miss Jordan, Sidney. And this is Mr. Conover."

Sidney bowed again and waved them farther into the dimness. He walked silently behind them down the long hall. It got darker and darker.

"Can you see?" Faye whispered excitedly.

"Of course not."

"I can," she boasted.

Along the gloomy hall on each side were irregularly spaced recesses with impressive round-topped doors. Only one of them was open and Sidney pulled it to swiftly as he passed it. But John Henry had gotten a peek inside. It seemed merely a sumptuous living room with low-slung furniture and a carpet as thick as the one they trod. The room was empty.

"If you please," said Sidney. Conover stopped short and the butler stepped ahead of him. It was the end of the lengthy corridor and there was nothing there but a heavy drape.

Sidney pulled the material aside and beneath it was another of the large curved doorways. John Henry rubbed his ear. The music had sneaked up on him. Beyond the door that Sidney was opening, a band was playing furiously, brassily.

The butler brushed by him again and John Henry had the impression that quick hands had patted over his coat. Faye squealed.

The stark fluorescent light that poured down from the ceiling of the room beyond blinded him at first. Faye's impetus sent him through the doorway and John Henry blinked around.

After the lonely gloomy entry the place was a shock. It was a big square room, low-ceilinged and almost completely functional. Occasional sporting prints on the beige stucco had been the only compromise with decoration. The complete absence of windows made the walls seem blind and faceless.

"Uh-huh," grunted John Henry as he began to catch on.

70

Near the door through which they had entered stood a bank of slot machines—stubby iron pillars from whose heads dials of lithographed fruit pictures peered. Opposite them were a series of chuck-a-luck tables with hour-glass cages of dice. Packed close down the center of the casino were faro and poker tables and at the far end was the long green board and dark disk of the roulette wheel.

"Isn't this fun?" Faye bubbled at his side. "Give me some money."

Automatically, John Henry dug a quarter out of his pocket. Though it was barely eleven o'clock, the wheel was in full spin. Men and women of all ages bordered the board. The card tables gripped another quota of gamblers, amateur and professional. Counterpointing the rhythm of the incandescent red juke box, an interminable hum of comment filled the room, punctuated by nervous laughs, the twittering of women and the monotonous drone of the croupiers.

The haze of cigarette smoke was being attacked by ceiling ventilators that sucked at it hungrily. Through the faint bright mist roved the excitement hunters, the wealthy visitors to Azure, dressed in the typical Azure garb of loafer suits, slacks and play dresses. The clothes seemed crassly out of place in a setting where tradition called for evening dress.

John Henry caught up with Faye. She was angrily shaking a slot machine a few paces away. As he looked around apprehensively for interference from the management, there sounded a violent click. Silver jangled.

"I won, Johnny!" Faye scooped a double handful of coins from the machine's torso. "Here's your quarter back. Yea, team!"

"Thanks," said John Henry wryly, wishing she'd lower her voice. "Now tell me, what's the big idea dragging me out here?"

"Aren't you having fun? I'm having fun!" Faye tried to find more pockets on her dress as storage places for her quarters.

71

"I mean, how did you know about this? Where'd you get that ticket that got us in?"

"Connections," she said and winked. "Only exclusive people like us get a magic card." Faye was skittish with excitement as she scanned the hall for new fields to conquer. "I met a cute fellow and talked him out of his."

She found her goal. "What you need is a drink," Faye announced confidently. She grabbed his hand and tugged him along an aisle between tables toward the polished wood and burnished metal of the bar across the casino. John Henry protested against what he knew was a bad idea.

"It's too early."

"Better early than never. What if we were struck by lightning?"

John Henry dismissed that conjecture and went along. He began rehearsing an explanation for Sin.

The bar was quasi-separated from the square gambling room by an archway which cut off some of the juke-box loudness. Its only lights were the pink neon facings on the big mirror. A solitary man hunched on one of the leather-topped bar stools. The mess-jacketed bartender was polishing glasses and softly whistling the opening strains of the Orpheus in Hades Overture.

Faye banged a small fist on the bar. The whistling choked off and the bartender blinked. "Yes, madame?"

"I'm buying. What'll you have, pardner?"

"I don't know. You order," said John Henry, avoiding the bartender's accusing glance. He hoped for something light and delicate.

"Two rye. Straight," said Faye.

Conover looked among the flushed faces of the milling gamblers in the main room. "What gets me," he mused, "is how they do all this. It's against the law, you know."

"But it's thrilling!" Faye chortled and snuggled up close, shivering.

John Henry edged away. "I'm surprised the police haven't

72

cracked down. Don't tell me they don't know this place exists." He grunted exasperatedly and spun around to the drinks on the bar. "Just what I've thought since last night—they're a bunch of crooked cops."

He looked in the bar mirror at the eyes of Lieutenant Lay.

"Morning, Mr. Conover," said the lanky police officer sardonically. "I didn't expect to see you again so soon." He sat beside John Henry, one stool removed. Close enough, Conover realized sickeningly, to have heard every syllable.

"Morning," he replied shamefully and seized the rye. Faye had already downed hers and was regarding Lay with interest.

She asked, "What's your racket, stranger?"

"This is Lieutenant Lay of the Azure police, Faye," said John Henry, digging an elbow in her ribs.

She giggled. "I like policemen. I never get a ticket." Faye whispered confidentially and loudly to Conover, "He's cute."

"Well," said John Henry nervously, "good to have seen you again, Lieutenant. Now, if you'll excuse us—"

"Don't run off," said Lay evenly and his tone made John Henry sink back onto the bar stool again. "I haven't seen you playing out there, Mr. Conover. What could you be doing here? Here, of all places."

"Go ahead, Johnny," Faye urged. "Tell him."

"It's very simple," he said. "I don't know."

"See!" Triumphantly, she downed the second shot glass of rye which the barkeep had quickly refilled. After a moment's consideration, she also drank Conover's fresh jiggerful.

"You wouldn't be figuring on following up Anglin's killing, would you?" asked Lay. He toyed with the tall glass of beer that glinted before him on the bar. The pink neon made his impassive face even more red.

John Henry's pulse raced. "Why? Do you think this is the place for it?"

73

"I didn't say that. I was just surprised to see you without your wife."

"Oh, she's back at the hotel."

"Convenient," said Lay and took a sip of beer. Speculatively, he eyed Faye Jordan, who was ogling the man behind the bar. "Most wives aren't that understanding."

The policeman interpreted Conover's quick frown of worry and chuckled. The bartender refilled the two small glasses again. But when John Henry reached for his it was already empty.

Faye winked elaborately at his surprised expression and spoke from behind her hand. "Better keep an eye on that bartender." She had a lot of trouble with "bartender."

John Henry sighed at the prospect of a drunken female on his hands in addition to everything else. Lay lifted his tall glass and said, "You better have one of these, Conover. They don't disappear so fast." He told the man behind the bar, "Draw a pale one, Herb."

Faye drew herself up and faced the police officer. "Lieutenant, do you have a warrant for my arrest?" She lost her balance. Her piercing shriek brought heads around in the gambling hall as she toppled to the floor in a jumble of bar stools. Her pocketful of quarters jangled like another jackpot as they spewed across the small room. The crowd clustered around the roulette table went back to their game.

"Did you hurt yourself, Faye?" John Henry asked, untangling the girl from the chrome-legged stools and helping her to her feet.

She was cooing happily to herself. "Play time," she gurgled. "Push me again, Johnny."

"I didn't push you—"

"Johnny! Where's my money? Where's my money?" Both Faye's hands scrambled in her dress pocket. "You stole it! I want a policeman!"

"For crying out loud, shut up!" said John Henry. "Your money's on the floor." He got down on his hands and knees

74

and began scooping it up. When he rose, red-faced, Faye was spinning contentedly on a stool, touching up her lipstick whenever she faced the mirror.

Lay's horsy grin was amused and mocking. He thrust out a long arm and handed a tall amber glass to the disgruntled young man. "Here. This'll get you on your feet."

Faye stopped shoveling quarters into her pocket. "I want to get on Johnny's feet, too," she announced and seized the glass for a long sip. "It tastes awful," she declared and gave the beer to John Henry.

Lay gazed through the archway at the midday turbulence in the other room. "Yeah," he said, as if continuing a conversation, "it's illegal, all right, Conover. But in a hopped-up town like this there's some things a cop has to keep his eyes closed about. It's not as if it was my department."

"Well, I don't know," John Henry doubted. "If people have passed a law—"

"I know how you feel." Lay consulted the circles of foam that swirled in his glass. "Compromises all the time. But if I got as rough as I'd like to around this burg, I'd be looking for a new badge. So I just do what I can." He looked at John Henry and smiled sardonically. "Here's to crime." He raised his beer.

John Henry put his own glass down empty and remembered Faye. The black-haired girl was in the front row at the roulette table arguing with the polite croupier. "I better go see what's happened to the problem child," Conover said. Lay toasted him silently with dregs.

"What's the trouble now, Faye?" he asked, elbowing up behind her.

"Johnny!" she squealed with delight. "I'm so glad you could come!"

"You brought me, remember?"

"This madman," explained Faye, gesticulating at the croupier who had halted his roulette wheel. "He won't let me play!"

75

John Henry raised his eyebrows questioningly. The croupier, a small dark man with a traditional thin mustache, put up slim and deprecating hands. "I have explained," he said plaintively, "But madame will not listen. A house rule—she must use chips. Not quarter dollars."

"Exactly," crowed Faye. "Sock him in the nose, Johnny."

The eyes of the crowd turned appraisingly on her selected champion. John Henry felt the blood coloring the back of his neck. He fastened determined fingers on Faye's soft shoulder. "Come on!" he gritted and propelled her away from the table toward the door at the far end of the casino.

Faye was giggling happily. "He's so strong," she said to the people they passed. "You have no idea!"

No one was playing the slot machines. John Henry halted there and spun the girl sharply around to face him. Her eyes got enormous and she weaved back and forth, hinged only at the ankles. "Now snap out of it, Faye," John Henry grated. He shook her gently. "I want a straight answer."

Faye straightened. She tried to salute but John Henry kept his grip on her arms. "You had a reason for bringing me out here. What was it?" he insisted.

"Wanted company," she crooned. "Faye's all alone."

"There's more than that."

Her eyes rolled from side to side as if she were watching a tennis match. Then her sleek braided head nodded slowly. "Gotta have words. Got something I wanna tell you," she whispered.

"What is it?"

Faye Jordan looked around cautiously. "Too many people. Everybody's listening."

"Okay. We'll go back to the car." Still holding Faye's left arm firmly, he opened the heavy door next to the slot machines and pushed her out into the dimness of the entrance hall. The closing door sliced off the light and the excited moan of conversation with one swift stroke. The mad pace of the juke box still sifted through, but softly.

John Henry put the concealing drape back in place. Faye had prowled away down the long corridor, opening doors and peering inside curiously. He caught up with her and said loudly, "Now what—"

She put a white forefinger across her lips. John Henry grimaced. The sudden change from glare to gloom made his head feel funny.

Faye opened the door to what appeared a combination library and den. Like the living room he had glimpsed on the way in, it was devoid of life.

"In here," she whispered.

He followed her in. The room was stuffy. John Henry went across to the open window that broke the wall of books. No air at all seemed to enter the library.

Faye had closed the door and was peeking back into the hall through the keyhole.

"What are you looking for?" he asked. The carpet tilted a little while he focused on her. He reached for the desk to steady himself and it moved away. Faye got up and walked toward him.

John Henry squinted. She was walking up hill and she got farther away. Then there were two of her, a dozen, a whole roomful.

He couldn't count Faye Jordan any more because all of her were performing a weird dance that glided around him, faster and faster. The last thing he heard was the chorus of Faye, giggling.

CHAPTER SEVEN

The radio's artful voice said, "This is KGB, San Diego's Don Lee station. Stay tuned for the San Diego Scrapbook with Gloria Winke. A transcribed announcement."

A tinkle of chords and a swing quartet broke into happy song.

> "For teeth that are whiter
> And quite a
> Delighter,
> (The cost is much lighter)
> Get brighter—
> Get BRY-TER!"

Sin flung herself across the bed and plunged the room into silence with a vicious twist of the knob. She was still panting with fright. And exertion.

Their clothes were scattered haphazardly around the bedroom. The two big suitcases yawned toothless on the bed. Sin had locked herself in the cottage and was obeying Sagmon Robottom's warning as quickly as possible. She gathered up an armful of lingerie and hurled it into the emptier suitcase.

When she picked up her husband's brown dress shoes, her lip commenced to tremble. Where was John Henry? It wasn't like him to dash off like that without a word unless— Sin's heart thudded faster than ever—unless he had learned something about the murder. Why did he insist on getting mixed up in things that were none of his business?

Sin wrapped the shoes in tissue paper she had saved from the unpacking the night before. Surely nothing could have happened to him in a crowded resort like Azure. Yet he was so dumb sometimes about the most obvious things.

The shoe wrappings rustled as she laid the package on her stack of slips. She caught herself watching the redwood desk in the outer room—the desk that held the Eversharp and the cipher. There was always the police. Sin turned her back defiantly on the telephone. If she started the police looking for John Henry and he was perfectly all right, he'd be angry about all the fuss. Nevertheless . . .

Sin was still pondering the question perturbedly when she heard a door close softly in the next cottage.

She got up off her knees from atop the suitcase, letting the straps slip free. That was Miss Jordan's cottage next door and if she had come back then John Henry . . . Eagerly, she peeked through the slats of the window blind.

It was not John Henry who had pulled the blue door to gently behind him and paused on the porch of Cottage 15. It was Gayner, his cadaverous face peering cautiously up and down the line of silent cottages. Then he stepped off the porch and started walking quickly down the flagstone path back to the hotel.

Sin opened the front door to her own cottage and stepped outside. Gayner had already vanished around a turn. Without reason, Sin began to run, anxious not to lose sight of him. Gayner was a tangible link between her and the tangled web that might have enmeshed her husband again. The assistant manager certainly was privileged to inspect the cottages whenever he chose—but something furtive in Gayner's manner warned her that this had been no official visit.

Gayner was just going through the glass doors into the Las Dunas lobby when Sin reached the sunken patio. She slowed her pace as she crossed through the gay umbrellas and lolling guests.

Somebody called her name behind her. Sin turned quickly, a hopeful smile beginning on her generous mouth. The

79

smile aborted. It was Sagmon Robottom, his bronze face stern, sauntering toward her from the pool. Sin whirled and fled. "Mrs. Conover!" Robottom called again.

She rushed up the steps and into the lobby. Gayner had gone past his registration desk without pausing and was now going down the front steps and crossing the driveway. His walk was brisk and purposeful.

"You look like you're in a hurry," Thelma Loomis said in her semimasculine voice, as the two women dodged around each other at the front entrance.

"Thanks," Sin said automatically and kept going. Mr. Trim was just getting out of the elevator. He lifted his straw hat high as if to beckon Sin closer. She gave him a tight smile and didn't slacken pace. Vernon laboriously forced the glass door open for her.

Gayner's brown-suited back was still in sight through the driveway border of palms and tamarisks. He was about fifty yards in the lead. This had been cut to twenty-five by the time the assistant manager reached Coachella Street. Sin loitered behind the concealing bole of a palm while Gayner looked up and down the peaceful street. Then he darted across and went hurriedly down the hill toward the center of town.

Near the corner of Cahuilla Street, a block away from the Las Dunas, Gayner sidestepped suddenly and disappeared from sight. Sin's pulse quickened but she made herself amble along in a tourist gait. If Gayner had realized he was being followed, she didn't want to appear suspicious. She could just keep going downtown.

However, Gayner was apparently oblivious of his tracker. When she reached the spot where he'd faded from view, Sin found he'd merely angled sharply into a narrow alley. As she walked past, Gayner was twenty or thirty yards up the alley, opening the back door of one of the buildings.

The place looked familiar and it came to Sin why it

80

should. Homer Anglin had died there. Gayner was letting himself quietly into the Ship of the Desert.

Gayner knocked on the door to Barselou's office. There was no reply, and the beat of his knuckles echoed emptily throughout the big deserted restaurant. He glanced back over his shoulder. Down on the main floor stood nothing but white-clothed tables, a flock of immobile sheep stabled in chairs.

He opened the door partway and edged around it into the office. It too was forsaken. The desk had been swept clean of papers. The tyepwriter on the metal stand in the corner squatted like a hooded falcon. Only a meager amount of the early afternoon sunlight seeped in through the closed Venetian blinds.

Gayner sat down behind the desk in the swivel chair and stretched. He found a cigarette in the center drawer, rolled a match from his vest pocket and scratched it into flame oh the sole of his shoe. Breathing out smoke, he pulled the telephone close to him on the desk.

The operator asked him to repeat the number. Then there was a humming of wires and then the measured cadence of the bell.

"Hello, there," said Gayner finally. "Give me Mr. Barselou, please." He took another long puff at the cigarette while he waited. "Oh—hello, Mr. Barselou. Gayner speaking."

He listened heedfully, nodding his head in agreement.

"That's what I wanted to tell you. I searched the Jordan girl's cottage." He listened briefly again. "No, sir. Nothing there. No, I'd swear to it." A smile slid over Gayner's pointed features. "Thanks, Mr. Barselou. I try to be thorough." Then, anxiously, "Are you any closer to the Queen?"

The receiver rasped irritably. Gayner's head bobbed up and down vigorously. "I understand that, Mr. Barselou. All the angles at my end are covered. We'll find her yet." The at-

81

tentive listening again. Then, "All right, I'll go through that one too. I'll call you later, Mr. Barselou. Yes, sir. Goodbye." Gayner replaced the receiver and sat in the striped light, silently meditating. Then he neatly punched out the cigarette's glowing stub against the rim of the metal wastebasket.

Sin peeked between the spines of a fan-shaped palm leaf. From her hiding place among the music racks on the bandstand, she watched Gayner come down the stairs from the second floor balcony and cross to the fiber tunnel that concealed the swinging kitchen doors. A moment later, she heard the faraway slam of the restaurant's back door.

To be safe, she waited as long as she could and then let out her breath. A church hush lay over the Ship of the Desert. Both the water and lights of the neon waterfall were turned off for the day. She was all alone in the dead restaurant. Sin began to feel more foolish than nervous. She had followed Gayner here without trouble—but what next? She'd have a hard time explaining to anyone, even an unbiased judge, what exactly she was doing trespassing. For that matter, she didn't even know herself.

Sin slipped down off the bandstand and tiptoed over to the twisted ironwork staircase that led to the balcony. Since she was trespassing anyway, she might as well make a good job of it. Wouldn't John Henry be disgusted if she found out something important and he didn't? Hugging the thought to her, Sin climbed the stairs, stepping carefully so her sandals wouldn't scrape on the tile steps. At the top, she paused to listen. She heard nothing to keep her from opening the door to the office which Gayner had just quitted.

The leather-paneled room was melancholy in the scant bars of sunlight that fell across carpet and desk top. Cigarette smoke still hung in the air and a thin thread flowed upward from the wastebasket, silent evidence of Gayner's recent presence. For some reason, the tobacco smoke gave Sin courage, adding a familiar note to the gloomy silence.

82

There was nothing interesting in sight, so Sin tried the desk drawers. They were unlocked. In the center drawer, under an open pack of cigarettes, was a sheaf of papers held together by a wire clip. She sat down in the big chair and liberated the sheets from the imprisoning clip.

The papers were all maps apparently of the area surrounding Azure, the Salton Sea and Borego Valley. The first one was labeled in ink: "Flood of 1849." Penciled under this was the handwritten notation, "Very rough reconstruction—prob. inaccurate." A large area of the drawing had been shaded, most of it lying south of Azure.

The next map was no more explicit. The date was 1891. Again a portion of the map was shaded but Sin discovered by comparison that the area was slightly smaller than on the first map, and more oval.

The date on the third map was 1905-07 and it was titled: "Formation of S/S." The familiar darkened area was present, but the topography was drawn in greater detail, with place names added. Sin recognized Highway 99 which they had followed north from Brawley to Azure. At the southern tip of the Santa Rosa Mountains, another and smaller section had been shaded, its vertical lines superimposed on the horizontal stripes of the larger expanse. A cross had been drawn in pencil at a spot in this area and a notation made.

The rest of the papers were heavier and glossier—aerial photographs of desert country on which she distinguished nothing familiar. She laid them aside and went back to the drawings with labels.

Sin squinted at the 1905-07 map in the brown light and then held it up to catch a little of the brightness filtering through the Venetian blinds.

Light, torrents of it, flooded the office. Sin shrieked and jumped up.

"Bad for your eyes, Mrs. Conover—reading in the dark," Vernon lisped. He leaned sorrowfully in the doorway, his hand still on the light switch.

83

Sin swallowed and tried to say something. All that came out of her dry throat was a croak.

Vernon moved toward the desk. Sin backed away, her hands outstretched to ward him off. The maps floated to the carpet. "I'll scream," she whispered.

Vernon shook his head mournfully and Sin saw for the first time that he was pointing a gun at her—a short gray automatic that matched the lapels and trouser-stripes of his maroon uniform. "Don't scream," he said, looking the happiest that Sin had seen him. "Keep quiet and you might be all right." He raised his voice. "All right."

Gayner stepped through the open doorway and regarded their captive with chilly amusement. "I hope we didn't give you too much of a shock, Mrs. Conover," he said pleasantly. "But you can understand we had to take certain precautions. Vernon, I believe you may put away the gun. Mrs. Conover realizes that she'll have to do as we say."

Vernon appeared displeased as he slipped the automatic under the tail of his tunic into a hip pocket.

"What do you want from me?" Sin quavered, her eyes darting between the two. Her lips were trembling so that it was an effort to form the words.

Gayner said heartily, "That's exactly what I was going to ask you. I'd be surprised if Mr. Barselou didn't repeat the same question. Don't make him repeat it too often."

"Start thinking up a good answer," Vernon advised her. "If you can."

Gayner motioned Sin courteously toward the door. He followed her out of the office and down the wrought-iron staircase. The young bellboy threaded a path before them among the empty tables and pushed through the swinging doors into the kitchen. The hiss of hinges and their footsteps were the only noises.

No one had mentioned John Henry, Sin thought. Was that good or bad? Well, she'd soon know. This would certainly be a lesson to her. She stepped high over the scrubbed

84

spot on the kitchen floor where Anglin's body had lain last night. It might be the final lesson.

"Where's the car?" asked Vernon. "I'll bet we don't have any keys."

"The usual place. I have keys," Gayner reassured him quietly. Before he opened the back door, "Now, Mrs. Conover, I needn't warn you that screaming or running or any commotion at all will be utterly useless. And very foolish on your part, I assure you."

They went out into the alley. Sin fought to grasp her dilemma. Here was not the terror of those frozen moments by the aviary when the white-haired savage had threatened her. The men walking on either side were not strangers. They were prosaic everyday persons—the assistant manager of her hotel and the bellhop who had brought her breakfast. Surely, Vernon in his ridiculous pillbox hat and overdecorated uniform couldn't actually kill her with that gun he carried!

Sin thought hard and said, "Wait a minute." The trio stopped. Gayner eyed her inquiringly.

Sin did her best to look tough and confidential at the same time. "Suppose," she said, "I was to spill it to you torpedoes and not to Barselou."

Vernon asked, puzzled, "What's a torpedo?" Gayner said, "Yes?" encouragingly.

"Well—" Sin groped for words. "If you got there first, you wouldn't have to split with the big boy." She hoped it meant more to them than it did to her.

"We certainly wouldn't," Gayner ruminated. "But, Mrs. Conover, can you give us the correct information?"

Sin nodded emphatically. "Play along with me and we'll all wear diamonds."

Vernon said, "I'm right for once." A smile nearly encroached on his freckled features. Then he confronted the other man bitterly. "You'll probably claim you've been thinking that all along."

85

"No," said Gayner. "You win." He prodded Sin toward the street. "I didn't think you knew anything, Mrs. Conover. Mr. Barselou was about to agree. I thought you were just a harmless snooper. But this puts a different light on it."

"You're going to take me to Barselou, anyway?"

"Definitely. You can make your bargain with him. As you quaintly put it, he's the big boy."

"But I really don't know anything!" Sin cried desperately. The dam of reason broke. Mounting waves of dread overwhelmed her. The men beside her were prosaic—but their matter-of-fact purposefulness was a gripping peril in itself. "I was just kidding!" She begged with wide shiny eyes.

"Come on," said Vernon. "I'm supposed to be on duty."

They urged her out into the white sunlight of Date Street. A few paces down the block, a sober black Buick sedan nuzzled the curb. The two men walked her quickly toward the car.

From behind them, a man's high-pitched voice called, "Yoo-hoo! Mrs. Conover!"

"You don't hear him," Gayner muttered and quickened his steps.

"Mrs. Conover!" Tires whirred on cement and Mr. Trim appeared alongside the trio, perched on a bicycle. Coming up behind him was the chunky figure of Thelma Loomis, also pedaling energetically. The Bry-Ter representative showed all his bad teeth in a waggish grin. "Ah, Mrs. Conover—you were trying to run away from me!"

"Not from you!" Sin choked.

Vernon and Gayner pushed against her from either side. Gayner said hurriedly, "We're in quite a rush, Mr. Trim, so if—"

Sin wriggled forward frantically. "Don't wait for me, Mr. Gayner. The streets are too crowded today for what you had in mind."

Vernon's hand strayed to the pocket under the tail of his tunic. Gayner's eyes were startled, but he said smoothly, "Oh,

86

we wouldn't think of going without you, Mrs. Conover."

"I've been wanting to talk to Mr. Trim, anyway." Sin put a hand on Vernon's arm, pulling the little bellboy's hand away from his hip pocket. "It was nice of you to offer me the ride."

Thelma Loomis got off her bicycle and grated, "I'm glad that's settled. You take this machine, young lady—I'm not built for it. I shouldn't have left the hotel at all, but Trim here talked me into it." She shoved the bike at Sin. "Here— or don't you think these things are safe?"

"Oh, yes!" breathed Sin, grabbing the handle bars.

Gayner bowed slightly. "We'll run along then, Mrs. Conover. I see we can't do anything to change your mind."

Sin couldn't do anything but shake her head.

Gayner smiled frugally. "Some other time." He jerked his head at the open-mouthed Vernon and the two got into the Buick. It slid away from the curb and turned the corner into Cahuilla Street.

Thelma Loomis clapped Sin on a trembling shoulder. "You and Trim have a good time." She strode chuckling up the street toward the Las Dunas.

Mr. Trim asked, "What was it you had to say to me, Mrs. Conover?"

"This!" Sin cried, laughing brokenly. Disregarding the straw hat he clasped against his chest, she threw her arms around the little man and kissed his bald spot resoundingly. "Mr. Trim, I love you!"

Mr. Trim looked solemn. "But what about your husband?"

"Whereabouts you want to go?" the truck driver growled.

John Henry frowned and then wished he hadn't because it made his headache worse. "Any place in town," he said. The driver eased his foot away from the accelerator and the huge freight truck slowed down for the 25-mile speed limit that began with the outskirts of Azure.

As the truck crept into the center of the city the vacant

lots and stucco homes became fewer. Here were shops, many of them branches of New York and San Francisco and Los Angeles stores, crowded close together and interspersed with neon-fronted and palatial nightclubs. Souvenir stands dotted street corners. Here and there, conspicuous in austerity, a branch brokerage office awaited the vacationing industrialist.

Few cars crawled the street today and only a sprinkling of people, although none of the stores observed Sunday as a holiday. Most of the tourists wore informal garb which was virtually a uniform in Azure—the men in shorts, slacks and T-shirts, the women in any of those, plus sun suits. Now and then this gaudy uniformity would be broken by the blue levis, plaid shirt and ten-gallon hat of a dude cowhand from one of the surrounding ranch resorts. Or the moccasined and brightly blanketed Indians who made their livelihood by posing for the eager cameras of Eastern tourists.

John Henry forgot his aching head for a moment as he got his first good look at the bizarre city. "What did you say?" he had to ask when he realized his burly companion had spoken.

"I was saying," the driver repeated ungraciously, "that you really see some characters around this place. Take a gander at that creep on the bike—a black suit in this heat!" His calloused forefinger gestured in disgust toward a couple approaching on the opposite side of the avenue.

John Henry followed the grimy finger. Then his eyes lit up. "Stop the car!" he yelled. Alarmed, the driver jammed on his brakes and the big truck and trailer screeched to a halt in the middle of Date Street.

"What the hell—" he was beginning.

John Henry had already opened the door and now he vaulted to the pavement. "Thanks a lot for the ride," he tossed over his shoulder and darted across the street.

"Sin!"

The red-haired girl on the bicycle looked up. Her eyes got

88

wider and wider. Then she put her hands on her cheeks and screamed. "Johnny!"

Her handle bars spun unguided into Trim's bicycle. Cement and sky whirled crazily for a moment. When the sky was on top for good again, Sin was sitting on the cement without a vehicle. Both bicycles were heaped near by on Mr. Trim.

"Sin, Sin—are you all right?" John Henry's voice said. Sin shook her head to clear it of everything except what she wanted most to see. Then she reached her arms up for her husband. He hugged her. She laughed against his shoulder.

"Johnny, darling, I was worried sick—"

"I'm sorry, Sin. I shouldn't have—"

"I was afraid—I didn't know—and those men—and the gun—they were going to—"

"You don't seem to be bruised," said John Henry, surveying her lovingly.

Sin put an experimental hand behind her. Then she sighed. "It won't show."

Amid a jangling of metal, Mr. Trim arose from the street to join them. His lower lip trembled. "Vicious!" he said and kicked the tire of the top bicycle. It rolled over lazily and impaled a pedal through the straw hat he hadn't picked up yet. He clenched his fists and drew ten deep breaths.

Sin began to get back some presence of mind. "I'm awfully sorry, Mr. Trim. I was so worried about Johnny and when I saw him—"

The Dry-Ter representative summoned up a brave smile. It faded quite a bit as he discovered one serge trouser leg was ripped from the hip down, exposing a milk-white thigh and calf. "They were new, too," he reminded himself.

"I'll insist on taking care of this," John Henry said.

Trim shook his head wisely. "Expense account."

Sin wrinkled her nose at the tangled bikes. "For real enjoyment give me a well-boiled icycle," she quoted.

89

The tooth-paste man looked puzzled. "That's a Spoonerism," explained Sin apologetically. "From Reverend Spooner of Oxford. He was always talking in reverse English. My mind's cluttered with useless quotes like that."

"Let's get out of the sun," Conover suggested. His headache was beginning to nag him again. Trim passed a palm cautiously over his naked scalp and agreed eagerly.

Across Date Street, the broad walk had been roofed over to shade the tables of a sidewalk café. They dragged the bicycles to the curb, sat down at the table nearest the street and listened to John Henry relate his adventures.

"I got dizzy all of a sudden," he concluded. "When I woke up I was all by myself in this empty library. Somebody had gone through my pockets. Faye was gone."

"She drugged you and searched you!" Sin said accusingly.

"I guess so. Anyway, I climbed out a window and walked to the main road and hitchhiked back here." John Henry looked uncomfortable. "All right, I made a fool of myself. Next time I'll keep my nose in my own business—like you, Sin."

His wife shifted uneasily and picked at a loose thread on her gay skirt. "Well," she murmured, "as a matter of record—" While she told of Sagmon Robottom and his mysterious warning, John Henry's chin began to jut forward. As she continued with the story of following Gayner and finding the flood maps, his face turned red. And when Sin had ended the tale of the near kidnaping, her husband slammed his fist down on the linoleum-topped table hard enough to bring a waiter scurrying out from the café interior.

"That does it! That's enough for us, Sin."

"What would you like, sir?" the waiter requested timidly.

"Nothing in this town!" John Henry roared, glaring at him. The waiter backed up and regarded him with bewilderment.

There was no amusement on Trim's face as he hunched across from the Conovers. He confessed slowly, "I don't

90

know what to say. My instructions never allowed for this sort of thing."

"We came here on a vacation," John Henry stated, and his voice was dangerously level. "Not to sun ourselves on a firing range. Not to be searched. Not to have my wife threatened."

"I'll admit that all this hasn't been very pleasant, but before you do anything hasty think of the Company that sent you here—free of charge. I feel personally responsible. What could I ever tell my Company?"

"Tell them to stop sending people to this munitions dump! We're through with it."

"Please reconsider. Please stay till tomorrow, at least. Until I can get in touch with the Company. I'll send a wire—"

John Henry sucked in his breath. He looked at his wife questioningly. "I'll leave it to you, Sin. You won this vacation. Do we go or stay?"

Sin spoke for the first time in several minutes. "We're already packed," she said.

CHAPTER EIGHT

M_R. T_RIM_ BADE them goodbye on the cement walk that led through the palms to the front entrance of the Las Dunas. Sin flatly refused to enter the lobby where Gayner or Vernon might be waiting. After a moment's thought, John Henry agreed.

So the Conovers sauntered innocently along the front of the hotel's south wing. Then, with a hurried backward glance, they turned the corner and plunged into the shrubbery that fringed the building.

"Do you think anybody saw us, Johnny?"

"Hope not," muttered John Henry. He pushed a path through the clawing branches for his wife. Trying to think out the best thing to do hadn't helped his headache any. The dangers of the morning—particularly to Sin—had sobered him more than he cared to admit. Last night, they had been merely bystanders to Anglin's murder. Today, they were virtually fugitives—possibly already marked as victims by some unknown hand.

"We'll get the baggage to our car and beat it," he outlined. "I'll phone what we know to Lay from some other town. The main thing is to get you safe, Sin."

Within view was the curving path which would guide them to the cottages. It was silent and deserted. John Henry held the last branches apart for Sin. The grass they hurried across was lifeless in the hot afternoon sun and lackadaisical bees sparred with the flowers. The flagstones leading up the canyon gave off ripples of heat.

Sin stopped in her tracks and squeezed his arm hard. "Johnny—look!"

Slouched on the porch of Cottage 14 was a familiar uni-

92

formed figure. It was Vernon. He was watching the path and his mournful face split into a pitying grin at the sight of the Conovers. He got to his feet.

John Henry hesitated only a second. Then he grabbed Sin by the elbow and whirled her around. "Back to the hotel," he said under his breath. "Keep going!" She had to quicken to a little trot to keep up with him.

"Gayner," she panted. "He might be there!"

"They can't do anything in the lobby. Not right there with people around."

"Honey, I'm scared!"

Vernon was matching them stride for stride. They reached the sunken patio. Sheltered beneath umbrella shade, two old men looked up curiously from behind their newspapers. There were no other loungers.

The Conovers pounded up the wide steps to the glass doors. They were halfway across the cool lobby when a thin length was framed on the front steps in the opposite glass portal. Gayner was just entering, his cadaverous face startled. His long arms came up, shoving the doors open.

Sin gasped out a little shriek. John Henry cast a lightning glance around. Except for the boyish clerk behind the mahogany counter, the lobby was empty. Both exits were blocked and the clerk was an unknown quantity. Without slackening pace, Conover swung his wife about and they headed at right angles for the elevator.

Gayner stepped into the lobby from the front just as Vernon clattered up the steps on the other side. The two men traded glances and started in pursuit of the fleeing couple.

John Henry half-hurled Sin into the open elevator. "Up!" he snapped and jumped in after her. He stopped in dismay.

"Johnny," Sin moaned, "there's no operator!"

His eyes rambled frantically over the control panel. The elevator was designed to function for either the individual guest or a professional operator, evidently depending on the time of day and the pressure of passengers. Now, the

93

determining lever was set in the drive-yourself slot. John Henry made up his mind in a split second.

He threw the sliding doors together just in time to avoid Gayner's clutching hands. Blindly, he pushed one of the black buttons on the panel. Machinery whirred, the elevator jerked and began to grind upward smoothly.

John Henry let out all his breath in a long shuddering sigh. His legs felt weak and he sought support on the operator's stool. He looked around at his wife. Sin was crouching in a back corner of the cage, her head buried in her arms.

"Buck up, honey," John Henry said as stoutly as he could manage. "We're doing all right." He almost added, "—for a while," but changed his mind.

The elevator came to a stop at the fourth floor. Conover heaved himself hastily off the stool and began helping Sin to her feet. She was trembling violently.

"It's okay, honey," John Henry said soothingly. He reached out a hand to open the sliding doors.

The elevator started down again.

Conover stood poised with one hand still outstretched as he fixed blank eyes on the control panel. The light marked "1" glowed an insistent red.

"What is it, Johnny? What is it? Are they going to get us?" Sin babbled by his side. Then he realized what was going on. When the elevator had stopped, Gayner or Vernon had pushed the "down" demand button on the main floor. Since the doors had been closed, the elevator had responded automatically to the command. Wildly, John Henry began punching at all the black buttons. The car continued its slow inexorable descent toward the waiting gunmen.

Sin began to wail in earnest as she recognized the despair on her husband's face. They passed the second floor. Next stop was the lobby.

Then, at the bottom of the panel, John Henry saw the red button. It was so conspicuous it angered him. He closed his eyes in enraged prayer and jabbed it.

94

The elevator jarred to an abrupt halt between floors.

Immediately, John Henry pushed one of the black buttons again. He shouted in exultation as the cage surged upward obediently. Laughing, he seized Sin by the waist. "We're still winning, sweetheart!" he cried. "Get out the minute it stops!"

Sin nodded silently, not daring to trust her voice.

The elevator stopped at the third floor. At once, John Henry forced the doors apart and they bounded out onto the lush carpeting of the hallway. As the doors slid to behind them the elevator clanked immediately and started down again. Apparently Gayner and Vernon still hoped to catch the Conovers in the cage.

"Where to now?" Sin asked tremulously.

John Henry pressed perspiring hands against his temples. The headache was gone. There hadn't been time for it. His brain wanted to operate in slow motion. They had momentarily baffled their pursuers—but what next?

"Can't we phone for help? Tell me what to do, please, honey!"

Sin's fright spurred his mind. "A call'd be stopped at the switchboard. Look—if we get separated, I'll meet you in the parking lot where our car is—"

"But our clothes—"

"The hell with our clothes! We'll send for them."

John Henry seized his wife's limp hand reassuringly and tucked it under his arm. They hastened down the wide hallway, looking from side to side for a friendly door. The rows of blank portals with discreet metal numbers were interrupted only by a stair well. At the end was a window showing the filigreed iron railing of the fire escape. "Where's Trim's room?" he wondered. "We might hide in there till they get tired hunting for us."

"I don't know," Sin said anxiously. "Maybe we should start knocking on doors."

John Henry halted by the stair well, indecisive. By the

95

window at the end of the hall, the last door opened. Sin wrapped herself around his arm so suddenly that he let out a yelp of surprise.

"Oh, Johnny—it's *him!*"

The man who stepped out into the hall was Sagmon Robottom. His white suit was natty and razor-creased. In one hand he carried a sun helmet, in the other his key. Every lean plane of his dark face went astonished as he sighted the Conovers. Then his features contorted sternly and he strode forward. The hand with the key plunged into his coat pocket and stayed there, a grim bulge at his side.

John Henry cut off Sin's incipient scream at the first syllable. He jerked her sideways and dashed down the carpeted stairs. Stumbling, gasping with renewed terror, she followed him in his wild flight toward the second floor. Ringing again in Sin's ears was the screech of tropical birds. Behind them, Robottom's flat shout trailed off and was lost in the curve of the staircase.

The second floor was exactly like the third—a deserted carpeted gauntlet of reticent doors. John Henry swung around the banister and took one heedless step down toward the lobby. Then Sin was clawing him to a stop. She backed up so quickly that she stumbled and sat down heavily.

In huge relief on the stucco wall of the landing was the shadow of a man climbing the stairs. A few more steps and the person himself would come into view at the turn of the staircase. The shadow wore a pillbox hat. It might be any bellhop. Or it might be Vernon.

With a squeak, Sin was on her feet again. John Henry hustled her along the hallway. The window at the end was a curtained view of the free outdoors.

"I can't go any farther," Sin panted as he half-carried her along.

John Henry had no encouraging reply. He was winded, too.

He fought the window sash up and stuck his head out.

96

The ground, a green jungle of matted shrubbery, was a long story below. His face brightened anyway.

"Out on the fire escape, Sin. Hurry!"

She scrambled awkwardly over the sill, inevitably catching her heel in the full peasant skirt. Swearing tensely, her husband followed. She clung to him on the grillwork platform. The long iron stairway was counterweighted to remain swung aloft when not in use. Sin's unreasoning fear of heights took precedent. She eyed the meager steps in terror.

"Johnny! I can't go down that thing!"

"Don't argue about it now. It's safe."

Her tentative foot tried it out. "But it moves!" she wailed. Down the hall, John Henry could hear Vernon's yell of triumph as he spotted the fugitives.

Conover delayed no longer. Seizing his protesting wife, he stepped out onto the swaying section of fire escape. It creaked rustily and the far end began to float toward the verdant ground. Sin's eyes were tight shut against her husband's lapel. Her hands clutched each other behind his back.

There was a clank and a slight bounce. The Conovers clattered down the iron steps and Sin made thankful noises when her feet reached solid earth. Freed of their weight, the staircase soared back to the second floor.

Vernon stuck his dour face out of the window above them and immediately withdrew it.

"The car—come on!" growled John Henry. They jammed their bodies into the yielding shrubbery. Oleanders clung to them with ardent hands, scratching Sin's bare arms and legs.

"Do you think we're safe, Johnny?"

"I don't know. Let's not stop and find out."

They trotted along the north wing of the hotel between a square-cut hedge and the stucco wall. When the hedge ended there was some more clawing shrubbery and then they burst suddenly into the Las Dunas parking lot to run for their car. The Chevrolet was beautiful in familiarity.

John Henry halted his glad reach for the door handle. He felt in his left-hand trousers pocket, then rummaged through all his other pockets. "Oh, no!" he said bitterly.

"What is it?" cried Sin.

"The keys. When Faye searched me, she stole the keys to our car!"

Sin let out a wail of fresh panic. John Henry peered into the useless sedan. The back seat cushion was askew and the door to the glove compartment hung open. The car, like their baggage and himself, had been thoroughly ransacked.

"Don't let them get me!" Sin's voice had a tremulo.

John Henry gnawed his lip and thought about using a hairpin to turn on the ignition. He gave it up. He'd never tried it or seen it done outside of movies and there wasn't time to experiment now. He pulled Sin aimlessly along the silent row of automobiles.

"Let's look for one with the keys in it," he snapped, trying to inject hope into his voice. Nobody in his right mind ever left his keys in his car—not these days—certainly not in Azure. "—den of thieves," growled John Henry, ignoring the nature of their present mission. The Conovers galloped down the double-parked row, glancing nervously in through car windows. They had rounded the row and were starting back toward the shrubbery on the other side when the shout came.

They stopped as if rooted. It was Gayner's voice and it came from the opposite side of the gallery of automobiles.

"Vernon," he was calling, "get a move on! They must be around here somewhere!"

Sin gave a little moan and sank toward the gravel as if her legs had melted. John Henry held her up with one hand. After a final look around at the unco-operative surroundings, he opened the car door nearest his hand—a convertible coupé with the top up—and thrust his trembling wife inside. He crept after her and shut the door quietly behind him.

"See 'em?" Vernon's question came from four or five cars away. Gayner replied something that John Henry couldn't make out. Sin was curled along the red-leather seat, breathing in little whimpers. He jabbed her with his elbow and put a warning finger to his lips.

"Okay," Vernon's voice came again. "I'll look over here, but it's no use."

"Johnny—" Sin began in a loud whisper.

John Henry jumped and turned cold. He jabbed her again. "Quiet!" he breathed.

"But, Johnny—" He scowled his blackest and she subsided, whispering, "All I wanted to say was that the keys—"

"Will you keep quiet?" John Henry listened for a shuddering second, then he whipped his head around. "What's that about keys?"

Sin pointed a finger. From the dashboard, a chain with several keys trailed down from another key which was half-buried in the ignition switch. The feeling surged over John Henry that he had been here before. He craned his head at the registration slip and his lips tightened. The name on the white slip of paper was Faye Jordan.

"I might have known," he muttered. Sin squeezed his arm. Gravel ground against gravel as shoes crunched closer to them. John Henry's breath was trapped in his throat. Somebody—either Vernon or Gayner or both—was coming slowly up the column of cars, probably peering into each one with gun ready.

"—forgive us our debts—" Sin was moaning into his ear, frightenedly. All John Henry could think of was that it tickled.

It was Vernon who spoke, and he was so close that the Conovers nearly fell off the seat. "I told you they went back to the cottage." Gayner's severe denial came from almost directly behind the convertible. John Henry's face bleakened. The trap was perfect now—the bellboy on one side and the

99

assistant manager on the other. Nudging Sin to move her hips, he cautiously wormed under the steering wheel and turned the ignition on.

The coupé jolted as a body leaned against it and a freckled hand trailed along the window ledge. John Henry made a lightning calculation and went into motion before his reason had time to argue. His right foot kicked at the starter. His shoulders shoved into view and he drove his left fist straight at Vernon's startled face. That amazed face, framed in the window of the convertible, drew back and the young man caught Conover's knuckles square in the Adam's apple. Vernon's profane surprise was just a squawk as he fell with a crash into the fender of the next car.

The engine exploded into life with a confident roar. Sin, hunched on the floor, was scrabbling for the emergency brake. John Henry threw in the clutch and the Mercury leaped forward, gravel spurting from its rear wheels.

Behind them, they could hear Gayner's thin voice, yelling. The coupé swerved to the right, cut around the parked cars and hurtled without a pause onto Coachella Street. At the corner, John Henry spun the car left and gunned off down Date toward Highway 99 and escape from Azure. The streets were still semideserted, with only an occasional stroller or bicyclist to break the somnolence of the midafternoon siesta. Sin pulled herself, grunting, to the seat. "Damn my memory. Damn my memory," she mumbled.

"Huh?"

"I'll never remember another thing as long as I live. I'll never go on the radio. I'll never answer a question in public. I swear it."

"You feeling okay, honey?"

"I guess so," Sin admitted grudgingly. She squirmed around for a last look at the hotel. "Johnny!" she squealed.

"Hurt yourself?"

"They're following us!"

The Mercury raced recklessly onto Highway 99. John

Henry flicked his eyes at the rearview mirror and swore definitively. A big black Buick sedan danced in the polished surface. It looked like Vernon behind the wheel.

John Henry glanced at the gas gauge and swore again, this time more collectively. The tank was less than a quarter full. They'd never be able to outrun the Buick on that. Before they'd gotten halfway to Brawley they'd be out of gasoline.

Sin didn't look at the gauge or the pursuing car. She studied her husband's frown. "What can we do, honey?"

"Let me think a minute," John Henry begged. He kept the accelerator flat against the floor mat. The shivering needle of the speedometer rocked past the black 60, heading for 70 with no hesitation. "Where the hell are the cops?" John Henry wanted to know, outraged. "Any other time they'd be swarming all over us. Don't they work on Sunday?"

Sin dared another glance back. The Buick still hugged the roadway behind them. It hadn't gained, but it hadn't lost any ground, either.

John Henry's cheerless face went suddenly incandescent. "The obvious thing!" he cried.

"What is it, honey?"

"The ranch!" he shouted. "There's a crowd at the ranch. They can't do anything to us in a crowd."

"But, Johnny, that's where—"

"Faye's back at the hotel—we've got her car. And Lieutenant Lay's at the ranch, isn't he? It's the safest place in the world right now!"

"You decide," said Sin in wifely fashion. "I'll do whatever you think is best."

The Buick seemed to be lagging behind. John Henry, keeping anxious watch in the rearview mirror, lost sight of the big black car for moments at a time as they raced up and down the rolling hillocks. The highway now curved slightly to the south. They were nearly to the dirt road which led to the Bar C Ranch. John Henry strained his eyes for the

101

small grove of fan palms and tamaracks that marked the juncture of the two roads. At last, he sighted it, rushing at them at seventy miles an hour.

Vernon and the Buick were hidden behind a rise of ground. He jammed on the brakes, easy at first, then harder. Tires screamed in protest as the convertible checked its headlong rush and slowed down to fifty. Black streaks of rubber lined the highway behind them. Sin sat with her eyes closed and her feet braced against the floor boards, awaiting the inevitable.

John Henry braked, gassed and swung the wheel simultaneously. The Mercury bounced off Highway 99 onto the dirt road. It skidded in the soft sand, swayed sickeningly for a moment, then righted itself proudly to shoot off at right angles to the highway. fifty yards off the pavement, Conover brought the coupé to a complete stop behind the screen of trees.

Sin peeked out from behind her arms. "Johnny! What are you stopping for? They'll—"

John Henry waved her silent. He was half-turned in the seat, watching what he could see of the main road through the back window. There was a furious rush of sound and the Buick sedan tore by them, its driver's eyes fixed unswervingly on the highway ahead. Vernon was alone in the car. Evidently Gayner had given up the chase.

Only when the black car had topped another hump in the ground and disappeared did John Henry blow out his breath. He grinned at his wife and let out the clutch again. The Mercury lurched forward over the uneven road. "I think we shook him for a while," he said. "By the time he finds out we're not in front of him, we'll be in safe company."

Sin dropped her shoulders back against the leather cushions. John Henry patted the closest portion of filmy blouse comfortingly and didn't say anything. By the time she raised a face that was white under its tan, the Bar C Ranch sprawled before the windshield.

102

"There it is, Sin."

"That's a nice house, honey," Sin said, her voice under control again.

They whisked under the log arch, up the driveway past the tamarisks and oleanders and came to a stop in the parking area. The drove of untended automobiles had vanished from the rocky pasture. "H'm," mused John Henry, "I hope the place isn't closed."

They didn't knock. John Henry had no admittance card and he didn't want to summon Sidney. The door opened easily, sliding silently into the dim foyer of the ranch house. The Conovers stepped in tentatively.

"I don't hear anything. You don't hear anything, do you?" Sin pressed the point nervously.

"It's in a back wing. That's where everybody is." They crept cautiously down the long gloomy corridor and John Henry pulled aside the drape. Then he felt happier. Through the heavy arched door to the gambling salon he could hear the familiar raucous song of the juke box and the clang of the slot machine just inside.

"We made it all right, honey!" he cried joyously, seizing his wife by one hand. He threw open the big door and plunged into the casino.

They stopped short on the threshold. The juke box was lit up crimsonly and blared noise of merrymaking but the great square room was empty of gamblers. All but one of the overhead fluorescent lights had been turned out. Felt covers had transformed the roulette and faro and poker tables into squat green mushrooms.

And two men remained of the crowd that John Henry had expected to mingle with.

"Well, look who came," said Barselou from where he stood before the one-armed bandit. He had pulled down the lever and the machine made buzzing sounds. It stopped whirring with a click and then a flood of quarters began to pour from the metal mouth.

"Jack pot," commented the other man and got up from his impromptu seat on a covered faro table. It was the plump waiter from the Ship of the Desert, but dressed now in a brown suit. In one fat hand he held a revolver.

CHAPTER NINE

"I DIDN'T expect you so soon," Barselou remarked. Unperturbed, he scooped up the quarters with one clench of his hand.

The pseudo-waiter was ogling Sin's tan calves. He gestured shortly with the gun barrel. "Come the rest of the way in. And close the door."

The stupefied Conovers obeyed. A metal panel swung open on the side of the slot machine. Barselou dumped the jack pot back in, closed the panel and locked it. He pulled the key from the lock and jerked his head at the fat man. "Better check the situation, Odell."

Odell advanced watchfully and patted John Henry's pockets and armpits and thighs with a questing hand. Then he looked at the girl and grinned lopsided. Sin shrank behind her husband and Conover clenched his fists.

"We won't cause bad feeling," Barselou told his henchman. Odell shrugged too late to be convincing. He moved away a few feet.

John Henry recovered his voice, though when he spoke it was scarcely better than a croak. "Lieutenant Lay?" he asked.

"Oh, were you expecting to meet him here?" Barselou asked suspiciously. When they didn't answer, he said, "It doesn't matter. He's been gone a good hour. Lay's a conscientious boy."

"Too conscientious," Odell put in.

"His bright idea was that we close down until the Anglin killing blows over. I didn't argue the point. Sidney and the boys deserve a couple days off."

John Henry mentally cursed himself for not heeding the warning of the empty parking lot.

105

Barselou waved them to the nearest circular table. "We might as well be comfortable." As the Conovers took chairs at the green-shrouded board, he said, "You see, the Bar C is more than a place of business to me. I like to know I can get up any time during the night and watch people making money for me. This is also my home."

John Henry couldn't suppress an audible groan.

Barselou sat in a chair opposite. The one fluorescent light which was alive shone directly overhead, erasing shadows unless a hand moved onto the felt cover. It threw Barselou's rugged face into high relief. Where his eyes should have been were black pits. Odell leaned against the slot machine, carefully inattentive.

"All right," said the big man. He was not deliberately unsmiling but, relaxed, his face was a cruel passionless block. "Now suppose we talk business."

"Okay," said John Henry, thinking fast, "we're willing to listen to a proposition."

Odell grunted. He was cleaning his nails with a match-stick. The gun had disappeared into a side coat pocket. Barselou looked more as if he were not smiling on purpose. "You don't catch on. You're in no position to bargain. We hold the cards, Conover."

"But not the Queen," Sin's small voice said from her chair.

"Don't let this room fool you," Barselou said coldly. "Gambling is for people who have to. This is my place— but it's not my way of life." From somewhere beneath the table, his hands came up with a deck of cards. They blurred in a shuffle and then he dealt the four top cards onto the green cloth, face up. Four queens.

"You see, I don't gamble," Barselou said. "You're right. I don't hold the big Queen. But I do hold you."

"That's a nice show," said John Henry. "I'm still listening."

"Then listen to this—I want to know everything that went on between you and Anglin."

"And if we don't feel like telling?"

106

Barselou nearly got up. Odell moved forward from the slot machine, his hand falling into his coat pocket. Sin grabbed her husband's tense arm and said quickly, "Wait! please wait a minute!" The men all looked at her. "Mr. Barselou, we have a confession to make."

"You came to the right church," said Odell.

"We don't know what all this is about."

Barselou laughed incredulously. The harsh sound died somewhere in the unlit reaches of the casino.

"That's right, Barselou," said John Henry with angry deliberation. "And furthermore, we don't want to know. All we want to do is get out of here and forget all about it. We were going home when we got sidetracked here."

Barselou shook his heavy head slowly. "That won't do. Not at all."

"Please, Mr. Barselou," Sin pleaded. "It's true. We're telling you the truth. We don't have anything you want. We don't know anything. Please believe us!"

A vision of a pencil in a desk drawer suddenly rose in John Henry's mind—Anglin's Eversharp that contained the long safe combination. He sneaked a guilty look at his wife, but her beseeching eyes were holding to their host. Either Sin had forgotten the pencil or she was using her feminine guile to throw Barselou a trifle off-balance.

"So you don't know what it's all about," mocked Barselou, considering them with narrowed eyes. "I don't swallow that, Mrs. Conover. You yourself told Gayner—"

"Please," Sin said earnestly.

A short stillness fell while Barselou turned something over in his mind. John Henry sat motionless, nerves taut, surrounded by the implements of chance. He fumbled with the beginnings of a plan, a gesture that might get Sin out of Azure, anyway.

Barselou had reached a conclusion. "Maybe," he said. "It's possible Anglin didn't tell you everything he knew. Maybe he didn't think you'd believe the actual facts about the

107

Queen. Or maybe you're lying. It won't cost me anything to refresh your memory. I want you to know what an unbelievable amount of money is at stake."

"You go a long way around," Odell complained.

"But I'm getting there," his employer said. He linked heavy fingers before him on the table and leaned toward the young couple. "The story of the Queen is quite a story, Mrs. Conover. If you've read any California history at all, you should know it."

Sin shook her head several times in denial. John Henry kept silent, prodding his brain. He had something to bargain with—the all-important pencil—but how to use it?

"In the year 1744, a Spanish galleon left Manila, headed for Mexico. This ship was loaded with valuables—jewels, silks, gold and other precious metals. The wealth of the Philippines, intended for Philip the Fifth. This ship was one of the Manila galleons that had been crossing the Pacific every year for almost two centuries. They came south along the coast of California and eventually arrived in Mexico— with luck. It was a hard trip, Mrs. Conover. It took several months and usually half the crew died of scurvy before they got to Acapulco.

"On top of this, there were other hazards. Pirates. They flocked from all over the world to get a crack at the Manila galleon. Sir Francis Drake, Woodes Rogers, Shelvocke, Clipperton—all of them had their try, one time or another. And there were plenty of others. They'd wait for the galleon in one of the harbors along the California coast. In 1744, this section of the country was unexplored. Then when the galleon came along the pirates would jump her. The battle was usually one-sided."

Barselou let his gaze encompass John Henry. "So the first point, Conover, is that the particular ship that left Manila in 1744 was named *La Reina*—the Queen."

"Okay," said John Henry against his wife's soft exclamation. "What does—"

108

"The Queen was commanded by a Spanish officer named Arvaez y Moncada. She carried a mighty rich cargo that year. To give you an idea, old records I've seen put the value of the pearls alone at four or five million dollars."

"Gosh," Sin murmured in an awed voice.

"An English pirate named Bledsoe fired on the Queen off the tip of Lower California. But Captain Arvaez was lucky. A storm blew up about that time and he was able to dodge the buccaneers. However, to be on the safe side, Arvaez decided to take the *Reina* north, up the Gulf of California. I guess he figured on waiting a few days until Bledsoe got out of the neighborhood.

"Well, the *Reina* sailed north, killing time. According to the old Spanish charts, she had reached the head of the Gulf. But as far as Arvaez could see to the north was a great inland sea. Neither he nor his navigator, a Portuguese named Ferrelo, had dreamed of such a body of water. But I don't suppose they were too surprised. In those days, the maps were more often wrong than right.

"Arvaez decided to explore this new sea. Ferrelo objected, according to what he said later, but Arvaez was the boss. So the *Reina* kept going north. Now and then they passed little islands but there weren't any signs of life. After several days, Arvaez discovered the sea was getting shallower. So he turned back to the south."

John Henry said, "What has all this got to do with us, anyway?"

"Don't rush me, Conover. You wanted to know details. The *Reina* headed south. Then Arvaez got the shock of his life. The way was blocked. The water had disappeared and only sand was left. Desperately, he sailed back and forth. Everywhere he went, the inland sea was drying up. At last, there wasn't enough water to allow the *Reina* to draw. Her keel struck bottom and that was that."

"I don't understand," Sin said slowly.

Barselou turned his shadowed eye-sockets on her again.

"Sounds like a bad dream, doesn't it? But it wasn't. Here's what had happened. There'd been heavy rains and this made the Colorado River overflow its banks. The overflow flooded this desert country, most of which is below sea level, anyway. The Queen sailed in when the flood was at its height. Then when the waters receded, she was left high and dry." He surveyed the Conovers' expressions of incredulity. "It's not only possible—it's fact. The same thing—the floods, I mean —has happened three times since that we have proof of. The last time was in 1905. That's how the present Salton Sea got there."

"Oh!" cried Sin excitedly. "That's what you were doing with those maps!"

Barselou's heavy lips curled ironically. "Brilliant," he murmured. "But let me finish the story. When the water was completely gone, the *Reina* was stranded in the middle of the desert. Arvaez and his crew were in a bad spot for sure. Hundreds of miles from civilization, a cargo worth millions and no way to get it out. No certainty of even getting out alive.

"They did what they could. Arvaez took a sighting. Then they packed up what they could carry and hit the trail for Mexico. Only one man made it—Ferrelo, the navigator. Indians or thirst took care of the rest. Ferrelo didn't much want to go back and look for the Queen, but he passed on what he knew about her. So during the next sixty or seventy years, several parties searched all over this section of the country for the lost treasure ship. But they didn't find her."

"How come?" John Henry wanted to know with sudden belligerence. If the Spaniards had rescued their ship it would have saved him a great deal of trouble. Possibly his life, the chilling reflection went on.

"Maybe Arvaez made a mistake in his sighting. Maybe Ferrelo's memory was bad. The important part is that the galleon stayed lost—until very recently. That's where you folks come in."

110

"You know where the Queen is now?" Sin asked unbelievingly.

"The general location, yes. From the dope I've gathered, I figure she's hidden somewhere in the Badlands. That's a section of desert between here and San Felipe Creek to the south. It's rocky, rugged country, chopped up with a lot of sublevel canyons that twist and turn every which way."

"If you know where it is, why don't you—"

"Because finding something in the Badlands is like looking for the needle in the haystack," Barselou replied coldly. "You can find it if you've got the time. I thought I had the time— until you showed up." His head tilted slightly so that his eyes caught the bluish-white light. The pupils showed as chips of silvered glass. "Now I can't afford to wait. From here on in, you help."

"What about Anglin?" John Henry insisted. "Who killed him?"

Odell flipped away the matchstick. His red eyes, hooded by puffy lids, gleamed. He said, "Why, you did, Mr. Jones."

"That doesn't matter," said Barselou impatiently, ignoring the shocked faces across the table. "Anglin's a dead issue. He doesn't interest me any more."

"Well, he interests me," said John Henry hotly, "particularly if it boils down to a mistake in our name."

"Which is not Jones," Sin added.

Barselou laughed suddenly. There was no amusement to be shared in the sound. "I hired Anglin last year to find the Queen. I was to pay him so much over expenses. A week ago, Anglin said he was on the right track. The galleon was somewhere in the Badlands and he was figuring out a route I could follow through the canyons to reach her, beginning at a fixed starting point which we agreed on."

"Oh!" Sin clapped her hands up over her mouth. The significance of the combination in the mechanical pencil had just come to her. John Henry nudged her under the table with a warning knee.

111

Barselou's chilly eyes watched the byplay. "Yesterday Odell found out that Anglin wasn't playing all his cards over the board."

"He thought he'd play it smart," Odell muttered and his mouth contracted bleakly.

"Anglin had wired to a Mr. and Mrs. Jones in San Diego telling them that he'd found the Queen. What exactly Anglin had in his mind, I don't know—perhaps he intended to force my price up. Or maybe he intended to collect from two people instead of one." Barselou's blunt nails punched into his palms. "However, Mr. and Mrs. Conover—or Jones—I will not play parlor games."

Sin protested faintly, "But we're not the—"

"We tried to get to Anglin before he saw you. We couldn't. So we tried to bluff you out. That didn't work either. Then —" he looked at Odell "—Anglin got himself shot."

John Henry said quickly and desperately, "You know we didn't kill him, Barselou. You were right behind me. He was shot in the back and fell into my arms."

"I can't remember, Conover."

"If you think we killed Anglin, then turn us over to the police—"

Barselou bared his teeth in what was meant to be a grin. "You don't get the point, Conover. I don't care who you are or what you've done. All I want from you is the other half of the puzzle. Anglin had only one thing that was worth a damn —and that was the route I need to find the Queen."

After a long silence, John Henry spoke. He said carefully, "I'm not saying we have the route, Barselou. But if we have— and hand it over to you—what next? The last guy that had the Queen information for you got killed at your door."

Barselou and Odell exchanged glances. The big man put a mask of friendliness over his granite features. "My lifelong policy in a rough business has been to avoid bloodshed. Give me the information, Conover, and your troubles are over. As soon as I've verified the dope, you're as free as birds."

112

John Henry looked at his wife, tensely upright in her chair.

"I know you won't go to the police," Barselou went on smoothly, "because if you did I'd have to tell Lieutenant Lay that there's a handprint in blood by the door of Cottage 15, which you occupied last night. Gayner saw it this morning. We think it's Anglin's blood. The police would be glad to test it for us."

Sin's eyes were big and hopeful and her dark-red tresses swayed back and forth across her shoulders slightly. "Okay," said John Henry.

"Now you're talking sense, Conover."

"Let me talk to my wife alone for a minute or two and I'll give you the route."

"You'll have to do your talking right here in this room," Barselou demurred firmly. "You don't get out of my sight."

John Henry rose and Sin followed him over to the chuck-a-luck tables along the side of the room. Odell had his hand in his coat pocket again. Sin whispered, "Johnny, what are we going to do?"

"Can you remember that combination, honey?"

"I guess so. You want me to tell them?"

John Henry shook his head fiercely. "Not on your life. Just do as I say." He rasped the top sheet off a long tally pad on the next table. Then he went back to Barselou. "Pencil," Conover said. The other man silently produced one.

John Henry took the equipment back to the corner where Sin was absently turning the wire dice cage. The tumbling cubes awoke minute rattling echoes in the still casino. "Okay," he muttered. "Start talking. Softly."

Sin closed her eyes, screwed up her piquant face and began whispering the combination to him. "R dash one. L dash three. R dash two . . ." John Henry wrote it down on his sheet of paper in small characters. "That all?" he asked when she paused.

"I think so, Johnny. I think that's all there is."

"Fine." John Henry tore the column of numbers off the tally pad sheet. He began folding the tiny strip between his fingers, refolding until only a small pellet remained. His brown eyes were very bright. "Now listen, redhead. I want you to do everything I say. Don't argue. Just remember I love you and do what I say. Got that?"

Sin acted dubious. "Well—"

"Promise me." John Henry squeezed her arm hard. "And remember I love you."

She smiled but her face was troubled. "I promise."

John Henry took her hand in his and marched her back to the two men under the stream of fluorescent light. Barselou hadn't taken his pale eyes off them. John Henry held the white paper pellet firmly between thumb and forefinger. "Got it?" Barselou queried.

"Uh-huh." John Henry held up the pellet. "This is it. I'm going to give it to you, Barselou—on one condition."

"Conditions yet," grunted Odell.

Barselou's black brows contorted dangerously. He said softly, "Yes. A condition?"

"That my wife be allowed to leave the ranch immediately."

"Oh, no, Johnny!" Sin cried.

"Shut up, Sin. How about it, Barselou?"

"Honey, I won't leave you!"

"How about it, Barselou?"

Barselou moved his eyes meaningfully to Odell's heavy coat pocket and said, "Why?"

John Henry popped the pellet in his mouth. Barselou didn't stir. He said, "So you swallow it. We know your wife has the information memorized. What's to keep me from letting Odell wring it out of her, Conover?"

Sin clung to her husband's arm. John Henry spoke carefully around the paper behind his teeth. "Don't make me discuss it at length, Barselou. My wife has a freak memory. Sure, she had the combination memorized. But once she repeats it, she can't remember it any more. And she's repeated

114

it. Anglin's dead, she doesn't know the key any more, and I never knew it at all. Your move."

"Nuts," said Odell and dropped his hand in his pocket.

Barselou waved a hasty hand at him. "Wait a minute," he said. "That'd be my first reaction, too, Conover. But, luckily for you, we've checked pretty closely on you two. What you just said jibes with something Gayner found out by talking to that writer—that Loomis woman."

"I still say nuts," Odell maintained.

"They couldn't have seen this coming up," Barselou said angrily. To John Henry: "All right. Suppose Mrs. Conover does leave."

"Fifteen minutes after she's gone, I'll give you the combination. And the longer we argue, the soggier this paper gets."

Barselou nodded his big head quickly. "You're free to go, Mrs. Conover."

Sin hugged closer to John Henry's arm. "I'm not going, honey!"

"Sin, you've got to. Don't argue about it. Nothing's going to happen to me with you loose. I'll be all right."

"I married you for better or for worse—"

"You also promised to obey me." Even under pressure, Sin managed a little smile over the family joke. "I'm ordering you to leave."

Her head drooped. "All right, darling," she whispered. "Please be careful."

He kissed her cheek and mumbled in her ear, "Keys are in the car. Go to the Brawley police station. If I'm not in front of it by six in the morning, go inside and spill the works." Aloud he commanded, "Now, scoot!"

Sin squeezed his hand and walked slowly to the door. He winked at her. "Goodbye, good luck and be careful, Johnny."

There was silence in the room for a while after the door had closed behind her. Then there was the faint sound of a car being started. The engine roared in the distance. Gears

115

clashed and tires whispered away on the gravel. The desert quiet returned again.

John Henry dropped his shoulders in relief and straddled a chair facing the other two men across the faro table. Their motionless eyes were glued to his throat muscles.

The three of them sat in the silence as the hands of John Henry's wrist watch crept from 3:15 toward 3:30. He shifted the wet paper pellet around to the side of his mouth. It was beginning to taste terrible.

Odell leaned back in his chair, eyes closed, a cigarette sagging from his lips. Barselou still sat directly opposite the door and his heavy finger pushed the playing cards around on the cloth in senseless patterns.

Conover broke the stillness. "How much will be left of the ship after two hundred years, anyway?"

Barselou folded his restless hands. "Probably not very much. But I'm not looking for relics. I want that treasure. And as soon as you hand over the route, I'll head for Walking Skull."

"What's that—the starting point?" Barselou didn't answer, so John Henry gulped a couple of times to make him nervous. Odell opened his puffy eyes and let the front legs of his chair come down to the floor.

"Fifteen minutes," he announced sleepily.

John Henry reached into his mouth and extracted the small wad of paper from it. Barselou stood up and stretched out an eager hand, but John Henry backed away from him toward the door, keeping the big man between himself and Odell. He reached in back of him, found the handle, twisted it. "Okay," he said. "Catch!" He tossed the pellet through the air at Barselou. As the hairy hands grabbed for the missile, Conover leaped into the protecting cover of the hall, slamming the door behind him.

Barselou forced the wet paper flat on the green felt before him. Then he smiled. Odell asked, "What about Junior?"

116

and indicated the fleeing Conover with a shoulder. Barselou shook his head amusedly.

From the front part of the ranch house there was the sound of a muffled crash, as if someone had dropped an armful of books. A moment later, the door opened.

"That does it," lisped Vernon.

Barselou jovially snapped his fingers at Odell. "Good work, Vernon. I think that takes care of the Jones situation. You better get back to the hotel now and tell Gayner he can stop worrying about everything."

CHAPTER TEN

John Henry moaned and opened his eyes. Gray light, like a shower of pins, stabbed them and he shut them again. A slow fire was baking one side of his face; the other was ice-cold.

"Johnny, Johnny!" he could hear Sin's voice near him. "Darling—please wake up—oh, please—"

He was lying on his side with one cheek pressed against dank concrete. He tried to sit up but his arms wouldn't come out from in back of him, and the exertion created bright pin-wheels before him in the darkness.

"Oh, darling!" Sin breathed from somewhere in back of him. "Thank God! I was so scared—"

His head began to clear. They were in some sort of dim vault under a low ceiling. Cardboard boxes of all sizes were stacked against the opposite wall. Down the center of the room ran a row of wooden pillars and, at eye-level above the cartons, were three small grimy windows. John Henry decided this must be the cellar under the Bar C Ranch. He sniffed the damp musty air and was sure of it.

"What's happened?" he managed.

"How's your head, honey?"

John Henry moved it gingerly to and fro. "God!" he complained. "What a headache!"

"Try to sit up. Maybe you'll feel better."

He discovered when he tried it that his arms were asleep. They were bound in back of him. His legs, too, felt numb and a moment's careful focusing showed him his ankles had been tied together and then his legs doubled back. A rope

118

connected his wrists with his ankles, this preventing any motion except wriggling.

He wriggled to a sitting position, groaning en route. There was something sticky on his lips. He touched it with his tongue and tasted the peculiar saltiness of dried blood. John Henry wormed around to look at his wife.

Sin had been similarly hobbled. Her red hair was mussed and her bright eyes had obviously held recent tears. She leaned one shoulder against the rough concrete wall, trying to take the pressure off her doubled-up legs.

John Henry groped for memory. "Sin—what are you doing here? Why aren't you in Brawley?"

"Your poor head, honey!" Sin exclaimed, ignoring the question, her eyes fixed on the lump which showed through the matted brown hair.

"Never mind me," he commanded, endeavoring to work some feeling into his arms by flexing his muscles. "What time is it, anyway?"

"I think it's been a couple hours at least since they brought you down here. Did they hurt you much, darling?"

"Just tell me what all happened."

Sin obediently repeated the gibing explanations she had gotten from Vernon when he had added John Henry to the basement prison. Vernon claimed the Conovers hadn't fooled him at all. When they had turned the Mercury toward Barselou's ranch, it had just saved him the trouble of an open fight. The bellboy had followed them quietly and listened outside the casino door. When Sin came out, he had shoved a gun into her spine and a cloth over her mouth. A few minutes later, she had been left, trussed, in the cellar—where she had been ever since. Vernon had then driven Faye Jordan's coupé around the drive and a short distance down the road to persuade John Henry that Sin had actually left.

The story didn't help John Henry's head at all. He sighed.

119

The near future was as gloomy as the cellar. Barselou might be keeping them locked up to prevent further interference. Or he might have other, and far more unpleasant, plans for the Conovers. John Henry was not cheered by the thought that he had not only set his own feet purposely in the danger zone, but he had also dragged his wife along with him.

Sin's thoughts strummed the same funereal note. The basement was too much like a tomb. "What do you think's going to happen to us, Johnny?" she asked fearfully.

"I don't know, Sin," he admitted gloomily. "It's all my fault. If I hadn't thought I could do better than the police—"

"It's not either all your fault," Sin said bravely, trying to control her trembling lower lip. "If I hadn't followed Gayner to the restaurant—"

"I should have left Faye Jordan alone. Then we wouldn't have come back here to the ranch."

Sin didn't argue about this. John Henry wriggled around a bit and whistled a noiseless tune between his teeth. He thought about Faye Jordan. "I don't think she knows anything about this ship business," he said suddenly.

"I can't see why you think that."

"I'm sure of it, Sin, the more I think about it."

"Well, then who was it that put something in your drink and searched you?" Sin demanded stubbornly.

"I thought it was Faye, all right. But why couldn't it have been that bartender of Barselou's? I thought it was Faye before I found out who owns this place."

"Why'd they let you go then, honey?"

"I didn't have anything. Barselou still wasn't sure we were the right people," said John Henry. "All that happened before you got caught with Barselou's maps. That put a clincher on our guilt. It made Barselou sure."

"But we didn't know anything," Sin protested.

"We had the route to the ship—that's enough evidence for him. It just goes to prove that there's somebody else mixed up in this race for the Queen, all right."

120

"Mr. and Mrs. Jones?"

"Sure, Sin. I don't know where Robottom fits in but he thinks we're the Joneses. Barselou thinks we're the Joneses. Anglin was looking for them when he stumbled into our cottage by mistake. Now who was he looking for?"

"Faye Jordan!" said his wife promptly.

"Look, baby—admitted that Faye isn't bright. Admitted she's wild. Admitted she's a lot of things. Okay. She hasn't done a single thing that makes us think she's tangled up in this murder, has she?"

"I don't like her. My feminine intuition tells me so."

"Let me make a point," said John Henry, after a pause. "There are two sides. Barselou on one and the Joneses on the other. Anglin was playing on both teams and didn't score anywhere. Barselou didn't kill him. So who did?"

Sin looked around at the shadows fearfully. "Honey, what does it matter, anyway? Can't we talk about something else?"

"Who killed him?"

"You want me to say the Joneses."

"Uh-huh. So the next big question is the Joneses. This is damned important, baby. Are they man and wife or a team of acrobats or what?" His charging sentences betrayed the struggle in his mind. "That's what we have to figure out. Fast."

"But, Johnny, what good is—"

"Sin, look. This is the point. Barselou thinks we're them. Our only chance in the world is to convince him that we're not. So start thinking, honey."

The fear she had been repressing broke from its hiding place with one dry sob. "Johnny—you make it sound more serious than—"

"It's liable to be, Sin. But don't think about that part of it." He tried to smile the worry off his own face. "Let's put that memory of yours to work in a good cause."

Sin nodded, bravely determined, and knit her heavy brows together. Only random scraps frolicked across her mind,

121

visionary odds and ends. Faye Jordan in her white knit bathing suit. Bry-Ter Tooth Paste. Thelma Loomis with her notebook. The sickening moments in the elevator. Sagmon Robottom's dripping wet body. Vernon's mournful eyes. Arvaez pacing the deck of *La Reina* while the water disappeared under his treasure ship. Who was Jones?

John Henry was staring blankly at the opposite wall. As if summing up a series of thoughts, he said softly, "It darn near fits."

"Did you think of something?"

John Henry pulled his eyes back to his wife's wildly hopeful expression. "Look, Sin," he said, "Jones can either be a man or a woman. Or both, I guess. Or several of either. Whoever it is has to be living at the Las Dunas, because Anglin was supposed to meet him there. It has to be somebody that isn't working for Barselou. Therefore, we can eliminate Vernon and—"

He stopped. A scratching noise came from one of the high windows in the cellar wall across from them.

Sin gulped a couple of times and whispered, "What is it, honey?"

John Henry shushed her gently and kept watching the ground-level window on the other side of the basement. A shadow blocked the remnants of sunlight on the dirty glass. The scratching noise came again.

Sin's face tightened and she gave a little moan of despair. She tried to wriggle closer to her husband for protection.

The window was being shoved firmly from the outside. It stuck for a moment, then screeched inward and upward. John Henry's mouth dropped open and he bumped his head in surprise against the concrete behind him. Sin gave a horrified yelp.

Crouched on the window sill, peering in at them curiously, was an animal. Behind a malevolent head with pointed ears, the creature's body filled the window. Its size made it

122

impossible for the huge beast to be what it was.

A gigantic black cat.

"Stand still—" Odell gritted between clenched teeth. The horse, intractable, shied away from him, flinging its head high and flashing the whites of its huge eyes.

Barselou laughed. "Give it to me," he demanded, taking the saddle from his henchman. "You got to know how to talk to them." He stroked the brown-and-white mare on the neck with one big hand and spoke soothingly in her ear. "There, there, Fern—nobody's going to hurt you."

Odell retreated across the stable and sat down on a bale of hay. From this safe point he lit a cigarette and watched Barselou skillfully slip the saddle over the mare's back and cinch it tight. He envied his employer's way with animals and wondered why he didn't have it.

"Throw me those saddlebags," Barselou called over his shoulder. Grunting, Odell pulled the empty saddlebags from their peg on the wall and plodded over to Barselou. The big man was leading another horse, roan-colored, from one of the stalls.

"You're being smart about a gun, aren't you?" Odell asked. Barselou smiled and pointed to the carbine scabbard lashed by the saddle horn. Then he squatted to cinch the saddlebags under the roan's belly. Odell walked to the sliding doors of the stable and looked out. A hundred yards away the ranch house was still and peaceful under the late afternoon sun, which now neared the Santa Rosa peaks. "Took too long getting your gear together."

"Oh, I'll find her in the dark okay." Barselou bridled the roan and led the two horses to the wide door of the stable. "I'm not riding blind with this." He slapped the watch pocket of his whipcord breeches. "And I'll be back some time after dawn—with souvenirs."

"How about those souvenirs in the cellar?"

123

"Just keep them on ice till I get back. But don't touch them, Odell—understand?"

"Don't worry."

"They better be in good health and able to talk when I get back. If they've given me the right dope, there'll be time enough then to shuffle them off."

"They're not going anywhere," Odell stated levelly. "But what if they've thrown us a curve?"

"We still got them, haven't we? Second inning, maybe we can persuade them to shoot straight."

"One thing," Odell said. "Let me have the girl, huh?"

Barselou put his foot in the stirrup and swung up to the saddle. He bent over and grabbed the reins of the pack horse. Then he straightened and stared down inscrutably at the plump man. "Okay," he said finally, "but women are going to be the death of you yet, Odell."

"Can't think of a better way to die."

Barselou grinned. "Walking Skull, here I come." He touched an unspurred boot heel to the mare and the horses began to move off in a slow trot. At the top of the rise south of the archery range, Barselou turned in the saddle and waved a hearty hand. Then he jogged out of sight. Odell took a final drag on the cigarette and pitched it out into the yard. He began to walk slowly back toward the ranch house. When he thought of the redheaded girl in the cellar, he started smiling.

The mammoth black cat poised on the sill and leaped lithely through the window to light on the concrete floor. Sin was drawn back against the wall as far as she could go, throat contracting in horror. John Henry blinked his eyes rapidly, trying to clear the monster from his vision.

Then the cat stood up on its hind legs. Without moving its jaws, it said, "For goodness sakes, what are you doing here?"

Sin commenced making incoherent little noises. The cat stepped closer and put a paw up to its nose. John Henry

124

grasped confusedly at a realization that the black fur wasn't fur at all but some kind of fuzzy cloth. The cat lifted its face off and the puzzled face of Faye Jordan took its place.

"Faye!" John Henry almost shouted. Sin gasped shudderingly and collapsed against the wall.

Faye Jordan said, "I didn't know you were going to come back, Johnny. I would have stayed if I'd known."

"Quick! Get a knife, Faye!"

"Where is that policeman and all the cute people?" She peered at the dark corners of the cellar.

"Don't waste time with questions!" Anxiety split the seams of John Henry's voice. "Find a knife somewhere and cut us loose, will you?"

Faye said to Sin, "He wasn't very nice to me this morning. Do you know what he did?" Sin shook her head mutely, green eyes fixed on the other girl's face expectantly. "He put something in my drink!"

"Oh, no!" groaned John Henry.

"You did too! And when I woke up in a closet somebody had searched me." Faye giggled delightedly.

Conover looked at his wife. His lips formed inaudible words: "She's—still—drunk."

Sin's expression was baffled as she considered the girl in the light of John Henry's mouthing. She murmured, "I don't know."

"I do!" exulted Faye. "And you should be ashamed of yourself, Johnny!"

"I am, believe me," John Henry said sincerely. "But now, Faye, please forgive me and cut us loose, will you, before—"

"How do you like my costume?" Faye asked, surveying herself contentedly. The big black ears flapped grotesquely. "It's for the ball tonight, you know. Are you coming?"

John Henry remembered then how Vernon had come to the cottage with the invitation to a costume ball—"come as what you'd like to be most," it had said. When had that been? Just last night?

125

"For crying out loud!" he shouted. "Turn us loose!"

Faye leaped back and Sin glanced angrily at her husband. She jammed a knee into his back and spoke soothingly to the girl. "How did you come to return to the ranch, Faye?"

"Taxi," said Faye and sat back on her haunches. "I'm glad you reminded me. I was trying on my costume and I decided to go for a drive, a fast one—to see what an ocelot felt like." Her face got unpleasant. "Then my car was stolen. Right off the hotel parking lot, too. I thought it might be here, so I took a taxi and hurried out to see. And do you know what?"

"What?" asked Sin fearfully.

"It's right here—just where I thought it would be!" Faye's short upper lip curled in triumph. She got up. "Where did you say those stairs went?"

"Faye, wait! Where are you going?"

"I'm going to find who stole my car—and then I'm going to kill him."

John Henry leaned an aching temple against the cement wall. Sin hunched forward and her voice was calm only by desperate effort. "That's exactly what you should do, Faye. But I've got a good idea. Why don't you untie us and then we can all look for the thief who stole your car?"

John Henry held his breath while the bright-eyed girl thought it over, afraid that a single movement on his part might turn the decision against them.

"That's a good idea!" Faye said after a minute of consideration. "I don't know why I didn't think of that. Here." She ran forward and kneeled at Sin's side. John Henry started to breathe again, but softly.

Sin gave a little cry and brought her arms around in front of her, free of the imprisoning ropes. Faye was unloosening the cords that bound her feet together. A few swift movements later, Sin pulled herself up. She swayed dizzily.

"How are you, honey?" John Henry asked anxiously.

"My fingers won't feel," replied Sin. "Just a second and I'll let you loose."

126

Faye Jordan was slinking around the pillars, a cat in every respect except that she prowled on two legs instead of four. She cocked the big ears to one side, listening. "I think I hear footsteps," she hissed. "I'll stalk them." She glided up the concrete steps, opened the door that led into the ranch house proper, and she was gone.

"Hurry up, baby," John Henry said nervously. "Barselou might come down here, especially if that screwball kicks up a rumpus."

"I'm hurrying as fast as I can," Sin whimpered, her fingers fumbling among the knots behind his back. "What's wrong with Faye, anyhow?"

"She shouldn't drink. There!"

John Henry brought his hands to the front and rubbed his wrists, trying to restore circulation. Then he brushed Sin aside and began to work his feet free. Sin went to the foot of the stairs, waiting nervously for some noise in the silent house above. John Henry got to his feet. Hundreds of black dots danced in the air. He shook his head and most of them went away.

He reached out and caught his wife in his arms for a brief hug. "We're all right now, honey! Keep your chin up," he whispered and urged her toward the window in the opposite wall. The grime-encrusted panes still swung half-open where Faye Jordan had left them.

"Can we get out that way?" Sin doubted. "It's pretty high."

"I can't see going up through the house again. We're taking the high road."

By piling the cardboard boxes against the wall, they achieved a perilous platform that threatened to collapse if they breathed wrong. John Henry scaled it first, wriggling painfully through the window and bumping his sore head on the frame. He scouted carefully. The window opened on the east side of the house, facing a small orchard of grapefruit trees. To the south were round, brightly colored targets on easels—an archery range. To the north was the front of

127

the ranch house and the parking lot. The afternoon shadows were long all about, but none of them moved.

He reached a hand down to Sin and pulled her awkwardly through the opening. She got up, straightening her peasant skirt and pushing her hair into place. North of the orchard, the barbed-wire fence was only about fifty yards away. Beyond that, cultivation ceased and sagebrush and scrub oak promised protective covering.

"Let's go!" cried John Henry and clasped Sin's hand tight.

They ran like mad for the fence, expecting a bullet in the back.

CHAPTER ELEVEN

AZURE HOTEL MAN BRUTALLY SLAIN

POLICE SEARCH FOR PHANTOM
KILLER IN SECOND WEEK-END
TRAGEDY HERE

Azure police this evening combed the city for a mysterious killer who has struck twice in twenty-four hours, following the discovery of the body of James V. Gayner, 35, assistant manager of the Las Dunas Hotel. Gayner was stabbed to death in one of the hotel's guest cottages early this afternoon, police said.

Lieutenant R. Fenton Lay, homicide bureau chief, claims that the murder is apparently closely related to the shooting of Homer Anglin, 41-year-old prospector, in Azure last night. Anglin, an Azure resident, was shot down by an unknown assailant a block from the Las Dunas Hotel.

A statewide alarm has been issued for the arrest of Mr. and Mrs. John Henry Conover, of San Diego, occupants of the cottage in which Gayner's body was found. The Conovers, present at the scene of the first slaying, have disappeared from the hotel. Lay announced.

"I expect an arrest within forty-eight hours," he said.

Gayner's body was discovered, stabbed in the back with a hotel letter opener, by Vernon Stebbins, 22, Las Dunas employee. There were no signs of a struggle. An automatic pencil, believed to be the property of the missing Conovers, was found beside the body.

Other hotel guests could shed no light on the double tragedy and police . . .

Not far ahead of them twinkled the lights of Azure, set in an incandescent halo against early evening. The burly driver turned a knob and twin beams leaped out ahead of the speeding truck.

"Whereabouts you want to go this time?" he asked wearily.

"Any place there's a phone," John Henry said, feeling a bit

129

embarrassed. He wished they hadn't flagged the same truck and trailer that had given him a lift earlier in the day.

"Drive-in up here has one. I'm going to pull in there for some chow, anyway."

"That'll be swell."

They bore down rapidly on a big neon sign that alternately flashed THE TOMAHAWK in red and then DRIVE INN in blue. Twenty-five yards beyond this, surrounded by a great circle of asphalt, squatted a round glass-and-wood structure, its ultra-modern resplendency typical of California roadside eateries.

The driver eased down on the brake pedal and pulled the huge truck and trailer off the road onto the asphalt. There he cut the engine and headlights. John Henry jumped down from the high cab and held up an assisting hand to Sin. She gingerly came to earth.

"Thanks for the lift," John Henry called up.

"Hey, buddy." The trucker's grimy face leaned over the vacated seat. He beckoned to Conover, who looked up at him suspiciously. "Just between us—what goes on, huh? I pick you up this morning by yourself. Tonight, I pick you up at the same place—but you got a babe with you."

"She's my wife." John Henry hoped this explained everything.

"Okay, okay," muttered the driver. "None of my business anyway." He withdrew into the dark cavern and opened the door on the far side of the truck.

"Gosh, am I glad to see people again," Sin burbled happily. "Just plain old unarmed people!"

"That driver thinks I'm nuts."

"Forget him, honey. We're just five minutes away from the police. Then we'll be all right. I feel like hugging Lieutenant Lay."

Only two cars nuzzled at the cement curbing before the glassy structure. Since the bulk of the evening trade hadn't yet made an appearance, the two carhops in blue striped

130

slacks and white blouses perched on tall shiny stools by the open front of The Tomahawk. Their make-up showed up garishly under the blue-and-white neon lights.

The phone booth was inside and at the far end of the counter. The room was almost deserted. The girl behind the counter whistled as she concocted a chocolate malt. The solitary customer was a pompous-looking man in his fifties who was reading a newspaper near the phone booth and munching absent-mindedly on a double-deck hamburger. As the Conovers came in, he gulped down the last bite, dropped a coin by his plate and squeezed by them.

John Henry pulled the folding door to the booth open and said, "I guess you just ask for the police."

"That's what it always says in the front of the phone book." Sin sat down at the counter next to the telephone booth and ordered two hamburgers—"with everything!" Then she reached out a bare arm and scooped up the newspaper the departed customer had been reading.

John Henry folded the door shut behind him and got comfortable on the built-in stool. He took the receiver off the hook. He listened for the buzz of the clear wire. He dropped the coin into the proper slot.

There was a sudden banging on the glass by his head and he reared back, startled. Sin was hammering one small fist against the pane and pointing to the newspaper.

"Operator," a precise voice said in his ear.

Sin was pointing to the top of the newspaper where it said *Extra!* in red ink. She shook her head furiously at him.

"Operator," the voice said again.

"Wrong number," John Henry answered mechanically and replaced the receiver. He pushed open the door, asking irritably, "What's wrong, Sin?"

"You didn't get the police, did you?" Sin grabbed his shoulders. Her face was white and strained.

"Not yet. Why?"

"Johnny—look at that!"

Her pointing finger trembled over the front page of the newspaper. AZURE HOTEL MAN BRUTALLY SLAIN. The tall black type blurred. John Henry shook his head, plopped on a seat beside his wife and, focusing carefully, began to read. His lips moved and now and then a phrase escaped. "Stabbed to death . . . guest cottages . . . state-wide alarm . . . arrest of Mr. and Mrs. John Henry Can-over . . . automatic pencil . . ."

"What are we going to do?"

"They think we did it!" John Henry gasped in amazement. "Can you imagine that?"

"But what are we going to do?"

He read the story again, rubbing his jaw irresolutely. This was a tight spot. Tighter and tighter. They were present at, perhaps implicated in, the first murder. Their alibi for the second murder was Barselou. And Barselou was certainly no friend of the Conovers.

Sin tensed, trembling. Hunger, weariness and confusion had brought her close to tears. John Henry took her chin gently between thumb and forefinger. "Calm down, baby. We're still going to shake loose from this."

"How? Johnny, they think we murdered those two men."

"Uh-huh. But we know we didn't. Don't forget that."

Sin cradled her head against his shoulder. "Why does everything have to go wrong?" her muffled voice wailed.

"There, there, baby. Don't attract attention—not now." The waitress was still whistling over the malt mixers, but John Henry noted nervously that the truck driver had joined them in the glass room. He regarded the Conovers with baffled curiosity.

Sin raised her head, rubbing at her eyes. "But we're all by ourselves, Johnny!"

John Henry slapped the counter and his face brightened. "We're not either all alone, not by a darn sight!" Sin's eyes stayed puzzled. "The prize—the quiz contest," her husband cried triumphantly. "Part of your winnings is a fairy god-father. He's supposed to take care of us and see that we have a good time, remember? He said so himself. Well, we're not having one."

"Oh, but honey—what can Mr. Trim do?"

"I don't know, baby. That's his department." Six seats down the counter, the truck driver was straining his neck trying to read the black headlines of the newspaper the Con-overs had laid down. "Anything at all would be an improve-ment."

John Henry banged the booth door to and began to call feverishly for the operator.

Thelma Loomis came out of the elevator, scanned the lobby hurriedly and then crossed the hall leading to the Oasis Room. It had taken her longer to put on her policeman cos-tume than she had expected. Now she'd have to make up for lost time.

The stiff blue coat with its shiny brass buttons felt awk-ward and strange to her and the trousers gripped tightly across the seat. She reflected again that costume balls were pretty silly and she'd never be going to this one if it weren't for business.

She paused in the doorway to sweep the room with keen eyes. Only two couples were dancing. Otherwise, the pol-ished floor of the Oasis Room was unmarred by scuffing feet. Less than a third of the glass-topped tables was filled, and their occupants, though in gay and indiscriminate costume, slouched lifeless and depressed. Mickey Mouse, ghost, Cleopatra, Roman senator, Robin Hood, satyr—all toyed with their glasses and manufactured desultory conversation for their companions. The scheduled laughter and bright chatter hadn't come off, save for one table in the corner where the Three Musketeers had toasted La Belle France too often.

Gayner's murder had flatted the hotel's note of cheer. In-

133

stead of fresh drinks, every table in the Oasis Room held a well-handled copy of the red ink *Extra!* edition of tomorrow morning's *Press-Telegram.*

The masquerading celebrators seemed content to nurse their highballs moodily and profitlessly and glance surreptitiously at other guests. Each eye seemed to mirror the suspicion that one of the costumes might hide the phantom killer publicized by the newspaper.

She couldn't see Sagmon Robottom anywhere. Thelma Loomis went on down the carpeted steps to the ballroom level and wound slowly among the tables to the wide doors opening onto the veranda. A man in a friar outfit fooled her for a second but she realized his shoulders weren't broad enough. Besides, the costume was hardly appropriate.

She stepped out onto the veranda. A few bizarrely dressed couples barred her path. She scrutinized them carefully and went down into the sunken patio.

Miss Loomis frowned and rubbed white-gloved hands together in perplexity . Then she ascended the steps to the glass doors and went through the lobby again.

"Three," she told the elevator operator. The girl looked around the lobby for more passengers and, finding none, closed the divided door. The car shot upward.

"Three," the elevator girl murmured and slid the doors apart. Miss Loomis strode down the hall past the stair well. Robottom's room was at the end of the corridor. No light showed under the door but she put her ear to the panel just to be sure. To be doubly sure, she rapped on it with a gloved fist.

Then she tried the knob. The door was locked. Frowning again, she turned and walked slowly back along the soft carpet toward the elevator.

The elevator doors came apart as she reached them. Two big tan-shirted policemen stared out at their spurious counterpart. They stepped from the cage in unison.

"Thelma Loomis?" the bigger one said.

134

She nodded.

"You'll have to come along with us. Lieutenant Lay wants to talk to you."

"This is about the right spot," John Henry said. The Tomahawk neon sign flashed in back of them up the highway. "I said about a hundred yards past the drive-in."

"Why couldn't we've waited for Mr. Trim back there?" Sin complained through the last mouthful of her hamburger. Eating while keeping up with the fast pace her husband had set from the drive-in had used up most of her breath.

"That newspaper," said John Henry briefly. He wiped mustard from his fingers and elaborated, "That driver was pretty suspicious. The minute he read that story he'd have hollered for the cops sure."

"Are you sure it's safe here?" Sin asked anxiously, trying to watch all the dark clumps of shadow at once.

John Henry thumbed toward a cluster of sagebrush which bulked beside the road. "Sure. We can hide back there till Trim gets here. I hope he has some ideas."

"Way back there?"

"I'll be with you."

Finally, Sin settled herself dubiously on a large flat rock behind the bushes. "I hope he hurries."

"I think he will. He sounded pretty excited when I talked to him." He cleared off the earth painstakingly and sat down. For a while they were silent, listening to the chirp of friendly crickets and the far-off hoot of an owl.

"Johnny—"

"Uh—huh?"

"What was he so excited about? I mean, he doesn't have a close personal interest in us. And if we were what the papers say we are, why, it's going to make the Bry-Ter Company look pretty foolish, much less their representative sort of shielding us."

"Sin," said John Henry after a pause, "don't think I'm

135

second guessing. But I was onto this same idea back in the cellar before that crazy Jordan girl leaped in and scared it out of me."

"Oh, it's just not possible, Johnny. I mean, how could he—"

"How could anybody? I don't know. But we're pretty sure this Jones person killed Anglin last night, aren't we?"

"Yes," Sin faltered. The owl hooted again, but it was no longer a sound of the peaceful night.

"And it must have been Jones who killed Gayner in our cottage."

"I suppose. Gayner would have no way of knowing we'd give the combination to Barselou. So I guess he went on looking for it. And found it, too, since the Eversharp was by his body. And Jones surprised him and stabbed him and got it instead."

"Well, why not?" demanded John Henry. "It's got to be somebody."

"But not Mr. Trim. He's such a nice little fellow. And just this morning he saved me from those two—"

"By gosh, it could all be part of an act." John Henry's voice took on a hard shell of excitement. "I think we've got something here, Sin. Who was it popped up right after Anglin stumbled into our cottage?"

"Well, he did know pretty much what went on with Barselou, remember—"

"And he was the one who said it was all right to move our clothes—"

"And, Johnny, if Mr. Trim thought we had the combination, of course he'd want to rescue me from Vernon and Gayner!"

"Honey," cried John Henry, his tone congratulatory, "for the first time, I think we're on the right track."

Sin shrieked and put her hands over her mouth. Her husband leaped to his feet, but there was no new menace in

136

sight. Sin rocked back and forth in alarm. "Johnny, I just thought—he's coming out here now. He's got the combination and he knows we'll guess eventually. He's coming out to kill us!"

"Good grief! I never thought of that." John Henry squatted behind the mesquite and beat one fist on his knee, trying to make a semblance of an idea take sensible shape. At last it did.

"For once this week end, we're ahead of the game, Sin. Look. You wait at the edge of the road for Trim to drive up. Nothing'll happen to you because he'll want us both. As soon as he's out of the car, I'll jump him. I'll be in the bushes—"

"I don't know, Johnny—"

"Why not? I'm a good fifty pounds heavier."

"But, honey," Sin reasoned, "what if we're wrong about him? What if he turns out to be just a nice little man and nothing else?"

"Then we apologize. It's simple."

"I don't think I'd laugh it off if you jumped all over me. And I didn't know you very well."

John Henry stood up and stretched. He felt better now that there was actually something he could do of his own volition. "Baby, that's a chance we have to take. We'll find out darn soon. From the story in the paper, it's obvious Jones got the combination."

"But—"

"And if Trim is Jones, he's not letting that slip of paper get out of his hands. He'll have it on him somewhere. So we'll search him for the answer." He checked. A sedan was coming slowly down the road from the direction of the Tomahawk. The driver was flicking his lights from high to low beam at regular intervals.

"Johnny, I'm scared!" Sin jumped up and put her arms around her husband.

137

"That's him, all right. Now don't be scared, Sin. Just do what I say and we'll be okay. Come on, now—show me what a brave girl you are."

"But I'm not a brave girl," Sin whimpered. "I'm *scared!*"

John Henry shoved her hastily through the mesquite toward the road. The automobile was almost upon them. It was slowing down. Tires bumped in the rough ground at the side of the highway.

"Is that you, Mrs. Conover?" Trim's high-pitched voice called.

"I guess so," Sin quavered. Trim turned out the car lights and shut off the engine. John Henry could hear a car door open and close, then the sound of footsteps crunching in the dirt, coming closer.

"Where's Mr. Conover?" Trim asked as he approached.

"He's—he'll be back in a minute," Sin stammered.

"Well, I certainly was worried about you two, Mrs. Conover, I don't mind saying," Mr. Trim was saying.

"Let's get off the road," Sin managed. "Here, behind these bushes—over here."

"Say, but I was relieved to get your phone call. I just knew you two couldn't be involved in what happened this afternoon," the little man continued. John Henry braced himself for the spring. Through the leaves, he could see the bobbing outlines of their two heads as they trudged toward him. Trim seemed to be wearing a three-cornered hat.

"We've been worrying, too," Sin said, glancing nervously toward the bushes. They were two yards away now.

One yard.

John Henry leaped like a tiger for Mr. Trim's throat.

The small man let out a yelp of pure terror and jumped backward. John Henry's hands missed the scrawny throat and fastened instead on a wide leather belt. The two men crashed heavily to earth and rolled toward the ditch. Sin was jumping up and down and shouting encouragement to her husband. "He's got a gun, Johnny! He's got a gun!"

138

Trim wriggled away and got up on his knees. John Henry tackled him around the waist again. A wizened hand scrabbled at the leather belt, trying to draw a long pistol from it. As though he had nothing else to think about, John Henry suddenly realized the significance of the cocked hat. Like Faye Jordan, Mr. Trim was all ready to go to the costume ball. He was dressed like a pirate, complete with skull and crossbones cockade on his hat. The long pistol was wood, with a cork on a string in the muzzle.

Trim brought the wooden gun up as if to use it as a club. John Henry's free hand snaked out and hit the other man's arm. The pistol sailed off harmlessly to clank on the running board of the car.

Sin screamed. Mr. Trim had slid away again and was scampering off down the road. John Henry loped after him and launched his stocky body into a flying tackle. The two men collapsed like a falling tree and slid along, face down in the sandy earth.

Sin ran up. "Johnny, Johnny," she was sobbing.

John Henry got up, panting, and brushed off his hands. "I'm okay, Sin. Lit right on top of him." Mr. Trim still lay crumpled on the ground.

"Is he—" Sin whispered.

"Nope. Just knocked out for a minute. He's still breathing." John Henry knelt and scooped up the limp figure in the pirate costume. "Come on." He strode back to the shelter of the mesquite. Sin tagged along, staying close behind. The moon, new-risen in the east, painted the scene in silver.

"I'll pass out his things, Sin. You go through them and look for the combination. Feel the linings especially."

"Hurry, honey—before he wakes up."

"Don't worry about that. Just make sure you don't miss anything," her husband said grimly.

He began to go through the little man's costume. Mr. Trim was breathing heavily, his mouth wide open. John Henry decided to start at the top and passed out the cocked hat for Sin's examination. Then, after quick arithmetic, he divided the task in half. Over the bushes to his wife, he tossed the long dark-blue coat and the bright-red knee-breeches. "That paper's pretty small. Feel carefully." On his side of the leafy barrier, John Henry searched the white ruffled shirt, the leather hiking boots with black oilcloth tops, the long white stockings, the shorts and undershirt.

The combination was not there.

"Find anything?" he called to Sin.

"Not a thing," she said, throwing down the wide leather belt.

"Maybe he wasn't hiding it. Let's look in the obvious places. Try his wallet."

"What wallet?"

"In his pants."

"There wasn't any."

"Maybe it fell out when I tossed them over."

Sin poked noisily around in the underbrush. "Here it is. I found it."

"Good," muttered John Henry and felt around inside Trim's boots again.

Sin let out a horrified cry.

"Find it?" John Henry burst through the bushes. Sin was standing by the car. She had turned on the parking lights to aid her search. In her hands she held a black-leather wallet and she stared at it with stunned eyes.

"What is it, Sin?" John Henry grabbed her arm.

She looked his way and her eyes got wider and wider. "Johnny, look at this!" Sin handed him the wallet. He took it and held it up to the light. Something gleamed back, something small and golden. It was a badge, and the lettering on it said FEDERAL BUREAU OF INVESTIGATION.

CHAPTER TWELVE

"Golmighty," said Mr. Trim.

Sin kept stroking his bald head with one soothing hand. His inert form had been clumsily redressed except for pirate hat and coat, and she kneeled on the ground, holding the bruised head in her lap. John Henry sat morosely on the running board of the gray sedan.

"I think he's feeling better," Sin whispered.

Her husband didn't answer. A vision occupied his mind, a vision of John Henry Conover gripping the bars of a cell while Sin pleaded with a relentless Trim about three stories high. He had assaulted and battered a guardian of the law and the law provided for actions like his.

"I wish we had a drink of something," Sin said, watching the face in her lap twitch.

"I could use it," John Henry answered emphatically.

"I meant for Mr. Trim. Sshh! I think he's waking up."

The pseudo-tooth-paste representative moaned again, stirred and rocked his head back and forth. John Henry leaned forward. Trim's brown eyes, more watery than ever now, opened and cleared. When he saw the two faces hovering over him, he tried to squirm away.

"It's all right, Mr. Trim," Sin comforted him, her hands holding his shoulders down.

"Let me up, dammit!" he croaked and spit out a mouthful of sand. Sin obeyed hastily, putting her helpful hands behind her back. Trim sat up quickly and then seized his head as if to keep it from rolling off his shoulders.

"Look," said John Henry, "I'll come along quietly."

This was not the greeting Trim had expected. He slid

141

along the ground a yard or two, got to his feet, and said, "Huh?" warily.

"It's all right, Mr. Trim," Sin repeated. "Really we're not criminals. Now that we know about you in the FBI and everything."

"Of course, it's out of the question to apologize. But if it'll make things any better, I'm sorry. Things just got moving too fast for us."

Mr. Trim wiped fine white dust from his face and considered them through narrowed eyes. He seemed taller. And when he spoke, his voice had dropped a full octave. He said, unsmiling, "Well, you stumbled into everything else."

"We didn't have any idea before we searched you," John Henry explained resignedly. "Your badge, I mean." He held out his wrists for the cuffs. "Here."

"Uh-huh. Just who the devil did you think I was?"

"Well, I figured—"

"No, Johnny," Sin spoke up. "We figured. You see, Mr. Trim, we thought you were this Jones that Barselou has—"

"Start from the beginning," Trim said wearily and sat down on the running board to hold his head.

· John Henry felt more and more like holding his too, as Sin explained the tenuous reasoning that had led them to believe that Trim was the mysterious Jones who was leagued against Barselou in the race for the galleon. It all sounded pretty thin now. "We thought we'd be smart and capture you first," Sin concluded.

Trim showed no surprise at the mention of the Queen or anything else. He just sat there, his brown eyes as hard as marbles.

"We're awfully sorry," Sin added weakly. "Does your head hurt much?"

"Never mind that," he said curtly. "I've had worse days. You've seen the papers, I suppose. Gayner's dead. Whoever killed him made off with the route to the galleon."

"We guessed that from the pencil," John Henry inter-

142

posed. "And that means two people know how to get there now." He elaborated eagerly, as if he were turning state's evidence, telling Trim how they had bargained with Barselou during the afternoon, lost overwhelmingly and escaped from the cellar with Faye Jordan's help. "Gayner's murderer is headed for the *Reina* right now, the same as Barselou. That's for sure. We thought you had the combination. That's why we searched you. I'm sorry."

Trim stood up and worked his shoulder muscles. "Where's the rest of my clothes?"

"In the front seat," said Sin, getting out of his way. "We're awfully—"

"I know," Trim snapped. He opened the car door and put on his coat. He donned the pirate hat at a rakish angle and jammed the wooden pistol back into his belt. Then he faced the fearful Conovers.

"Very well," he said, "we'll call it quits. You probably thought you were doing the best thing and you haven't exactly gotten in the way—yet. Besides, as the Bry-Ter Toothpaste man, I haven't been any great help to your vacation."

John Henry thought it wise to keep silent. But Sin asked, "There's really supposed to be a tooth-paste man here?"

Trim grimaced. "Yes. I'm taking his place for a while—a deal the Bureau cooked up so I'd have a good reason for wandering around town. As you've found out by now, Barselou's got it pretty well sewed up."

"You're after Barselou?" John Henry burst out.

Trim sat on the edge of the car seat and stared down at him. After a while of consideration, he went on. "I'll tell you what I can, but you two have to be frank right back at me. In answer to your question: only incidentally. There's some tie-up there with Sagmon Robottom and—"

"What's he done?" cried Sin.

"Nothing yet—that we can prove. He just keeps popping up in key positions. A professional organization one place— a crackpot discussion group somewhere else. The L. A.

143

office—that's Robottom's home town—thinks there's something off-key about him."

"Off-key?"

"Subversive. Undercover."

"Gosh," said Sin, awed. "If I'd known that, I'd have really been scared this morning."

Trim pursed his lips irritably at the interruption. "Nothing had come of my work when I ran across this lost treasure business. Okay—that's not my jurisdiction—finders-keepers and so forth. The two murders aren't my jurisdiction, either. Just a minute!" He held up a small hand to cut off the Conovers' questions. "I do come into it sideways. If Barselou finds the Queen, the money's his. But the government is interested if he's going to back Robottom in some subversive activity with that money."

John Henry began to pace back and forth, plucking thoughtfully at his lower lip. "Then Robottom could be Jones?"

"Oh, he could be," admitted Trim. "But the two dead bodies belong to Lieutenant Lay—not me. I'm here to cinch a subversion case. All I know about your Jones or Joneses is that a Barselou employee—Anglin—sent a wire to them yesterday morning. That's all I got from the telegraph office and I was too late to find out who picked it up at the San Diego end."

"But how about us?" Sin wanted badly to know.

"Oh, you're clear. San Diego cleared you this morning."

"I know we're not spies, too!" cried John Henry. "Just being murderers has got us worried!"

Trim scratched his pug nose. "Yes, I can see that Lieutenant Lay may be a little hard to deal with, being up the tree he is. I have some unpleasant memories of local authorities myself. However, once the killer is found, you should have no further trouble."

"That may take months." John Henry hurled a stone viciously across the highway.

144

Sin screwed her face up pitifully. "If you couldn't be Jones, why couldn't you just be the real tooth-paste man? We need help!"

"It is too bad," Trim said. "The Company wasn't supposed to send their winners here this month. I wasn't much help to the last couple, either. No one was more surprised than I when that writer woman told me you'd arrived last night." The agent laughed for the first time since John Henry had jumped him. "My dear young lady, for someone who's been playing detective, your guesswork's way off. Do you think a tooth-paste company would choose a representative with bad teeth?" He gaped to show his.

"Well, I didn't know," Sin protested. "I didn't know what their old tooth paste would do. I always use salt!"

Trim chuckled, his good humor apparently restored. "I'll do this much. I'll do what I can with Lay tomorrow morning. I'm sorry I won't be able to run you back to the hotel, but from what you've told me, I better get a move on." He started to slide under the steering wheel.

Sin looked at the agent quizzically. "What are you going to do now, Mr. Trim? Or is it a secret?"

"Well—" Trim squinted at the moon-painted mesquite. "I'm going out and wait for Barselou at his ranch. Now that you've run this galleon rumor to earth for me, I might as well warn him about registry and tax and some other details. Then it'll be his move if he wants to play with Robottom."

"Couldn't we come with you?"

John Henry looked up sharply. "What did you say, Sin?"

Trim frowned whimsically at the girl. "Hardly. You'd just be in the way for sure, Mrs. Conover. Besides, I'd imagine that the Bar C was about the last place on earth you'd care to go back to."

"It is," said Sin earnestly and grabbed the little man's hands. "But, Mr. Trim, look—wouldn't you like to follow Barselou and Jones and Robottom or whoever it is to the Queen? That way you could—"

145

"What are you talking about, Sin?" John Henry interrupted. "I thought you—"

"It has its points," Trim mused. "I might find out pretty definitely about the subversion angle. It would certainly catch Robottom off base." He laughed harshly. "But, unfortunately, Mrs. Conover—I don't know the way. All I can do is wait at the ranch for one or both of them to come back."

"That's it exactly," said Sin, jumping up and down with excitement.

"Sin, talk sense," John Henry insisted angrily. "We've got enough trouble without borrowing any. Let's get back to town and start looking for a good lawyer."

"Johnny, don't you see? We know where to start—Walking Skull."

"What do you mean we know where to start? Where's Walking Skull?"

"Never mind," said Trim quietly. "I know where it is. Let her talk."

"And we've got a third copy of the combination—me." Sin pointed a proud forefinger at herself.

John Henry was disgusted. "Don't be silly. You've said it once. Now it's gone. Why should that list of numbers stick with you?"

"Because," Sin explained slowly and deliberately, "they don't make sense!"

"She hasn't had much to eat," her husband said to Trim.

"No, Johnny! Just to prove it, here's the first two directions. R dash one. L dash three." Her words tumbled over one another getting out of her mouth. "I know I can remember it, Johnny. It just isn't a silly old quotation or anything—it doesn't have any order and I can remember it perfectly. I knew it when I recited it for you back at the ranch, but I didn't want to tell you then for fear it would spoil things or you'd want to go after the Queen by yourself later on. But now we've got help. And, Johnny, honest—I can't get the darn thing out of my head!"

146

"It'd be too dangerous for you, Sin. I don't want you—"

She put her arms around him. "I don't want to go to jail and I don't want you to, either. This way we won't have to, honey. Because Jones will be at the Queen."

"But aren't you scared, honey?"

"Uh-huh. I'm scared to death. But I want us rid of this horrible thing. The only way we can be is to find Jones."

John Henry felt the tempting excitement begin to bubble inside him again. "I wouldn't mind running into the guy responsible for all this, at that. I feel I owe him something."

Triumphantly, Sin turned to the wizened agent in the sedan. "There! Now how about it, Mr. Trim? What do you say?"

Trim didn't say anything for a moment. He opened the glove compartment and took out a heavy service automatic. Leaning back in the car, he checked the magazine under the dashlight. When he came into view again, he shoved the gun at John Henry, butt foremost.

He said, "Stick close to your wife then, and come along. This may be the bag of the year or it may be a wild-goose chase. I guarantee it won't be any picnic."

The tan-shirted cop pounded loudly on the door to Cottage 14. Then he opened the door and motioned Thelma Loomis into the room ahead of himself and his companion.

She scanned the room coolly. Every light in the cottage had been turned on and the air was hazy with cigarette smoke. The desk, the wastebasket and the area around the doorknobs had been dusted with a gray powder. Near the desk, the carpet bore the dark oval of dried blood like a seal.

"Wait here," one of the policemen said, and they went into the bedroom. Voices wandered back out to her. Miss Loomis fished in the unaccustomed pocket of her blue patrolman uniform and brought out a package of Fleetwoods. She was lighting the cigarette with a steady hand when Lieutenant Lay came in from the bedroom. His brown suit was

147

wrinkled and his horse face was hemmed about with tired lines. He still needed a shave.

"Thelma Loomis?" he asked heavily. The blonde woman nodded her helmeted head slightly. Lay motioned at a chair and sank into the one opposite. His eyes studied her keenly. Thelma Loomis worked her lips and a smoke ring came out. Then she crossed her legs without hitching up the knees of her trousers.

"That your real name?" Lay asked suddenly.

"Don't you know?"

"Don't be smart. I asked you a question."

"It's my real name."

Lay nodded. He pulled a brown imitation-leather notebook from his inside coat pocket and flipped a couple of pages. Then he looked up. "You say you're a writer?"

"That's right."

"Work for *Fan Fare*. Campbell Publications."

"That's right."

Lay closed the notebook and shook his head. "That's wrong. We checked with Campbell Publications this evening. Want to see the wire we got back?"

Thelma Loomis grinned. "Never mind."

"Okay, then. Suppose you tell me who and what you really are, Miss Loomis. Campbell says they never heard of you or anybody like you."

The blonde woman took another slow drag on the cigarette. "If you want to know what I really am, check the Castle-Scudder Detective Agency in L. A. They'll tell you. So should this."

He looked at the plastic-sealed card in her wallet and handed it back. "Private cop, huh?"

"Yep. Except the movies say shamus, Lieutenant."

"Glad to know. Let's have the whole story," Lay suggested and closed his eyes to slits as he leaned back in the chair.

"It's nothing you haven't heard before. Errant-husband stuff."

148

"Who's the victim?"

"Sagmon Robottom. The archaeologist. You've probably talked to him by now—and he probably told you plenty about himself. What he didn't tell you was that he walked out on his wife a week ago. Myra Robottom. Now Myra's not the gal to take that sort of thing lying down."

"Jealous?"

"Sagmon's quite a hand with the girls. It's been going on too long but now Myra's gotten tired of it. Last week—the old last straw. Sagmon dashed down here without explaining and Myra's sure there's another woman involved. She's pretty upset but if there's to be a divorce it's to be Myra who gets it. So here I am."

"What have you got?"

"Nothing that'll stand up in court—yet. But I'm getting warm. There's a gal here at the hotel, name of Faye Jordan, that Glamor Boy thinks is hot stuff. She's playing him on a line right now. But it's just a question of time."

"At twenty bucks a day. God, women!" said Lieutenant Lay scathingly. He opened his eyes again and rubbed his unshaven jaw.

"I was looking for Robottom when your men put the arm on me. It's my guess that he's off somewhere with the Jordan dame." Thelma Loomis uncrossed her legs. "Now that I've shot square with you, Lieutenant, how about giving me a break and letting me go back to work?"

Lay got up. He smiled bitterly. "You're about as square as a tennis ball—all you private cops. But go ahead, get back to your keyhole." Thelma Loomis grinned and nodded thanks, no trace of resentment in her impassive face. "Oh, by the way," Lay added, "since you're looking for Robottom—" He paused tantalizingly.

"You know where he is?" the blonde asked eagerly.

"The man I got in the lobby says he grabbed a taxi this evening and said something about going out to the Bar C Ranch."

149

"Good." Thelma Loomis rubbed her white gloves together. "Good."

Trim moved a hand to the horn button and turned off the car lights. Then they rolled slowly down the incline toward the rambling shadow of the Bar C Ranch. Beyond the gallows-like archway, the low ranch house showed no lights.

"Looks like Faye's still here," Sin said, speaking in an unnecessary whisper from the back seat. The Mercury still lowered inanimate before the house. The only cloud in the sky had floated mischievously before the moon, a cottony mask.

Trim coaxed the sedan to a quiet halt. He ceased listening to night sounds from the surrounding desert. "Still want to go through with it?" he inquired.

"Sure," Sin said, pretending she meant it.

They opened the doors and got out. John Henry caressed the automatic pressed against his stomach. He tried to remember which button was the safety. He recalled too distinctly his most embarrassing army habit—during the one or two practices he'd undergone with firearms—of pressing the safety catch and watching the magazine plummet to the ground. Wisely, John Henry merely patted the gun butt and left it alone.

Trim led the way across the graveled lot. The cloud chose to drift from in front of the moon and the three furtive figures seemed to spring into focus. Sin was regretting her insistence on the expedition. Her white blouse made a distinctive target under the gleaming moon.

When John Henry veered toward the front door, Trim caught his sleeve with a quick hand. He shook his head. "Never mind stirring up trouble we don't have to. Where are the horses?"

"The stable, I suppose."

"Can you two ride?"

150

"Well—we've ridden."

"Lead the way," said the Federal man and stood aside. Hoping he was going in the right direction, John Henry tiptoed cautiously along the front of the silent house and turned the corner. He was. The boxlike building, a half-story higher than the house, loomed in sharp outline a hundred yards away.

Trim nodded approval and brushed a finger across his lips. The trio started the long, exposed march from house to stable, pausing every other step to inspect the ranch house and listen for alien noises. As they entered the square black shadow cast by their goal, Sin let out a shivering sigh of relief.

"Now," Trim began, "if we can—" He made a convulsive movement. His boot heel landed on John Henry's toe, and Conover doubled over groaning. Sin froze next to him, wide-eyed.

Something white fluttered in the gap between the sliding doors of the stable.

"Everybody just stand where they are," Odell said, "and don't make any sudden moves."

He came plodding from the dark slot, the barrel of his .32 shiny over his fist. John Henry forgot his bruised toe.

"Imagine," Odell said pleasantly. "Mr. and Mrs. Conover, back again. Who's this?" He swung the revolver toward the little man.

"My name is Trim."

Odell wasn't impressed. His plump shoulders shook with inner laughter. "I figured somebody'd be along, just as soon as I heard Gayner got his." The evening was not cold and he'd taken off his coat and tie. The white shirt seemed disembodied above the brown trousers. "Looks like I was right."

"Where's Barselou?" John Henry asked. "There's some questions—"

"Forget it. But let me tell you, Junior, I'm mighty happy

151

you got back before he did. I wasn't looking forward to explaining that rope trick, believe me." His blood-shot eyes canvassed Sin. "I'm glad you came back, too."

"Johnny—" Sin's voice shook.

Odell gestured with the gun. "Okay, turn around and put your hands on the back of your head." He peered at Trim. "What the hell kind of hat you got on, anyway? Go ahead—turn around." They faced the ranch house. Behind them Odell's voice said, "Now start walking. Not too fast."

The three head-clutching figures began to walk slowly back across the moonlit yard. Sin shifted her head enough to see her husband's tight-lipped profile. "I'm sorry, Johnny," she murmured.

"Keep moving," Odell said. "And cut the talk." He coughed.

They marched forward in silence. Nearly to the ranch house, Sin glanced quickly to either side of her. Trim and John Henry were intent on where they were walking. But strain her ears as she might, Sin couldn't hear any footsteps behind them. Maybe that was because of the sandy ground. She wondered if she dared peek around. Gritting her teeth, she lowered her hands cautiously from her neck, braced for a possible blow.

Nothing happened. Emboldened, she looked back. Then she whirled, grabbing at the two men. "Look!" she cried. "There's no one following us—"

"Where'd he go?" asked John Henry, astonished.

"Let's get out of here before he comes back!"

Trim's small arm clutched her in mid-flight, held her back. "Don't worry, Mrs. Conover. He's not coming back." His finger pointed. Just outside the stable's square shadow was a mound of dark and white. Something like a furled pennant stuck up from the sprawled figure.

John Henry ran toward it. Trim and Sin followed. Nearly there, Conover checked, turned and pulled his wife against

152

his chest. "No. Just look the other way for a while." A moment later, Trim rejoined them. His humpty-dumpty face was grave in the moonlight.

"Dead," he said quietly.

"But how did it happen—no noise—" Sin gulped.

"He was hit in the neck by an arrow. Death must have been almost instantaneous. Paralyzed him, maybe."

Sin remembered Odell's cough and shuddered. John Henry's arm tightened around her shoulders. "Pretty lucky for us," he said soberly, "though I guess that's a kind of a horrible thing to say."

Trim said, "Save your sympathy. He didn't deserve anything better." He glanced at Sin's trembling form. "Think about the otherwise."

"Where—who could have shot the arrow?" she asked.

"There's an archery range around at the other side of the house," John Henry said. "Saw it this afternoon, coming out of the cellar."

"That's where it came from, then," Trim ruminated. "Want to take a look?"

"I guess so," said John Henry reluctantly. "What'll we do with Sin?"

"Not a thing, Johnny. Where you go, I go."

"Stay a little behind us, honey." He pulled out the .45 as if he knew just what to do with it.

The archery range was empty. Nobody lurked out on the sparse grass behind the targets. Far off, a coyote howled.

Trim opened the coffin-size box against one side of the ranch house. "Unlocked," he said. "Could have been anybody."

The arrows were loose in felt-lined canisters on the floor of the outdoor closet. One space was empty in the rack that clamped the unstrung bows against the wall. Someone had leaned the last weapon carelessly within the archery cabinet and its cord was still taut from tip to tip.

153

The agent lifted it out and tested the pull idly. It was a hickory longbow, taller than he was. "All longbows," he commented. "Try that."

John Henry took it and plucked at the cord. To bend the bow slightly required most of his strength. "I guess Barselou's a pretty powerful guy."

"I guess somebody else is, too," said Trim and replaced the bow. The coyote howled again.

"Let's get away from here," Sin quavered.

Disturbed, the three hurried back to the stables. Sin gripped John Henry's fingers and managed not to look at the crumpled body mercilessly floodlighted by the moon.

The horses in their stalls were restless. They tossed their heads and reared and neighed when the men approached. Sin huddled on a bale of hay by the doorway while Trim and her husband first pacified and then saddled three mounts. John Henry had a good deal of trouble subduing his steed, but the wizened FBI man proved surprisingly adept at the job and finished two saddlings while John Henry struggled with one.

Trim carried the last of the saddles and bridles into the feed room and banged the wooden door to behind him. Then he wedged the huge rusty padlock shut and jammed it with one blow of an old stirrup iron. "That'll slow up anybody who's going our way," he remarked, his smile satisfied. He tossed the stirrup iron down and dusted his hands.

They swung silently onto their horses and moved out into the moonlit yard, the erect little pirate leading. Sin's white blouse had lost all crispness and a shoulder seam was threatening to part. Her bright full skirt was wrinkled. It kept hitching above her knees every time she changed position on the saddle. John Henry's sport clothes looked no better.

The crunch of hoofs on the sandy ground was the only sound, but at the archery range Sin reined in and reached

154

out a hand toward her husband. John Henry halted his horse. "Huh?"

After a minute she put on a faint smile. "It's all right. For a minute there, I thought I heard a sound—like somebody trying to call."

Her smile faded and she kicked her horse in the ribs. "Too much imagination, I guess."

CHAPTER THIRTEEN

"THIS IS Walking Skull," said Trim. "And that's the start of the Badlands." He gestured into the night.

The Conovers looked it over. Walking Skull was a rough bowl-shaped depression in the desert, several hundred yards across. It was littered with huge boulders and dotted with a few stunted palms.

"Why?" Sin wanted to know.

"Good thing the Bureau made me into a guide book before I came down," Trim said. He explained that a weathered skeleton had been found leaning against one of the rocks years before, looking as if it were still trying to take the few steps that separated it from the tiny water hole. Of course, the bones were all gone now—carried home as souvenirs by tourists. But the skull had never been discovered. "The legend is that the skull still roams these parts at night searching for water."

"Oh, no!" Sin said.

"You shouldn't have told her," was John Henry's reaction.

To the south and to the west, the smooth desert had been carved into a twisted labyrinth of narrow, deep canyons, writhing snakes that turned here and there, joining and separating and losing themselves in the night shadows. A single canyon cracked the side of the rough bowl on the southwestern edge.

"I can see why you'd need a combination to find your shadow in a place like this," John Henry observed. "I feel lost already."

"That one canyon that cuts into Walking Skull—that must be the starting point. From then on it's up to your wife."

"How about it, Sin? What's the first move?"

156

Sin wrinkled her tan forehead and concentrated, summoning the long list of R's and L's up before her eyes. On the ride from the Bar C Ranch, they had all agreed that these must stand for right and left and the number indicated the canyon to be followed.

"R dash one," she announced triumphantly.

Trim nudged his horse forward and the Conovers followed. At the mouth of the canyon that led from Walking Skull into the Badlands, the pirate hat was outlined briefly and ludicrously against the sky for a moment. Then Trim disappeared between high sandstone pillars into the shadowy chasm. His voice echoed back, over the clip-clop of horses' hoofs. "We turn right at the first cross-canyon. You still agree?"

The Conovers agreed in an echoing chorus. The dark jagged walls rose higher and higher on both sides. They rode down an incline until the sky was a crooked slit of comparatively pale blue overhead, then the canyon floor leveled somewhat.

"You still all right, honey?" Sin called over her shoulder. John Henry lurched in his saddle while his horse missed its footing temporarily. He hung onto the saddle horn and said, "Just dandy."

"Here we are," Trim announced. "I'm turning right."

Sin's eyes were becoming more accustomed to the reduced light. She could see the bay rump of the lead horse as the little man reined it into the first side canyon. Vegetation was sparse and scrawny in the gully they traveled. The floor was sand and smooth stones of all sizes. At the sides leaned great sheets of shale that had evidently crashed down from above. She looked up nervously. "How do we get back out?" she yelled to the man ahead of her.

"Follow our own trail."

"Can you see Barselou's tracks?"

"I can't see much of anything," Trim replied cheerfully. "But three horses kicked things around more than one. And

157

we'll be coming back by daylight. What's the next turn, Mrs. Conover?"

It came to her easier this time. "Left three."

"John Henry bumped along reflecting on the sandstorm that might obliterate their return trail. Trim had requisitioned their only canteen from Barselou's stable. Three emaciated bodies, hopelessly lost in the tangled canyons . . . vultures . . . whitening bones . . .

He grimaced and tried to forget the legend of Walking Skull.

Thelma Loomis turned her spotlight up on the timber archway and read the twig letters carefully. Then she clicked off the spot and urged the car forward up the curved driveway. The Bar C Ranch house was dark, a somber bulk in silver moonlight. She braked the automobile in front of the door. On the parking lot were two cars—a convertible coupé and a gray sedan.

Miss Loomis moved quickly. From her big plain purse, she dug out a snub-nosed silver revolver. Expertly, she flipped the cylinder out and examined the shiny brass shells protruding from every socket. Satisfied, she eased out of the car and stuck the revolver in the wide belt of her policeman uniform.

Her flashlight beam probed over the other two cars, then swung back to the gloomy house. Thelma Loomis walked the length of the low porch slowly, her practiced feet making only the faintest noise on the tile. Above her hung dark stalactites of bridles and branding irons. Nothing stirred.

"Uh-huh," she murmured and clucked her tongue thoughtfully. Ignoring the brass knocker, she punched the button beside the door and stood listening to the distant loneliness of chimes. When the last tone had died, she tried the latch. The heavy door swung away from her on oiled hinges. Her flashlight cut a round hole into the blackness beyond. Lightly, she stepped after it and closed the door behind her.

158

John Henry squinted at the luminous dial of his wrist watch. It was nearly four hours since they'd left the Bar C Ranch. The moon was directly overhead now, melting the shadows at the bottom of the tortuous canyons.

He stood up in the stirrups and tried to find a more comfortable position.

Sin twisted around on her horse, her tired face pale in the moonlight. "Something wrong, honey?"

"I was just wishing this horse and I would have a meeting of minds," he called. "We've met every place else."

Beyond her, Trim halted his horse and said, "Not so much talking, please. If Barselou hears us—"

John Henry lapsed into moody silence. The constant prospect of sheer canyon after sheer canyon was monotonous. He punched a knee into his horse and it stopped. "I meant giddap, Nightmare," he said wearily and tried a heel. He came up alongside the other two riders.

"You do think we must be nearly there, don't you, Mr. Trim?" Sin was asking anxiously.

The Federal agent was indefatigable. He sat erect and alert in the saddle, apparently as fresh as when they had ridden away from the ranch house. His narrow shoulders shrugged under the blue buccaneer coat. "I hope you can answer that better than I can, Mrs. Conover. How many more numbers are there?"

Sin pushed her eyes shut and put her hands to her cheeks. She felt wrung dry. "I don't know," she confessed finally. "Two or three, I guess. They just seem to come one at a time."

Trim pushed his cocked hat back farther on his bald head and grinned encouragement. "Didn't mean to hound you. Guess I'm getting a little worn down myself. I keep worrying over what the office would say if they could see me now. What's next?"

"Right one," Sin replied automatically.

Trim flicked his reins and began to move toward the next

159

gap in the high stone corridor. The Conovers trailed after him. Sin drooped in the saddle, her hair bouncing at every lurch of her horse. Her husband put over a comforting hand and stroked her shoulder. She lifted her head and smiled wanly at him.

For a while after they made the turn into a new chasm, there was no sound except the clip-clop of hoofs and the occasional swish of a tail. A spark enlivened the gloom now and then as an iron shoe glanced off rock. The walls, oddly carved by the wind, towered almost a hundred feet over their heads.

Trim reined in. He tilted his pug nose upward, sniffing. Sin whispered, "What is it?"

"We're getting close," Trim muttered.

"How come? Whoa, Nightmare!"

"Do you smell anything?" The Conovers sniffed tentatively. "I caught a whiff of smoke just then. Campfire."

"Barselou?"

"Maybe." Trim sucked air over his teeth. "Or Mr. Jones."

John Henry's sleepiness disappeared as excitement hit him like a cold shower. Sin's eyelids quit drooping. "Im scared," she said needlessly.

"The horses make noise enough. I don't have to warn you two to be quiet from now on."

"I'll say you don't."

The FBI man straightened in his saddle. "What's the next one, Mrs. Conover?"

Sin squinted studiously. The number seemed to elude her. "Left—left—two," she said doubtfully.

Trim's horse plodded forward.

They passed the first gray mouth of a canyon on the left. Sin caught her first scent of burning wood. Despite the danger it presaged, the familiar fragrance abated her nervousness. There was other human life in all this desolation.

She frowned suddenly. They had passed the second left-hand canyon. Sin cupped her hands beside her mouth and

160

called after the little pirate softly. Trim wheeled his mount around and rode back. John Henry caught up with them once more.

"What is it, Mrs. Conover?"

"You've made a mistake," Sin explained. "We passed the second canyon just then."

"Oh, that," deprecated Trim. "You were the one who made the mistake—not I. Your memory's phenomenal, Mrs. Conover. But that last direction should be 'left three,' not 'left two.'"

He dropped his reins on his saddle horn and opened his fist. Lying in the palm was a strip of oiled paper, a narrow curling strip of directions which began, R-1, L-3, R-2 . . .

Sin's lips moved but no sound came out. John Henry's mouth hung open loosely.

With his other hand Trim plucked the wooden pistol from his belt. He let John Henry stare at the cork on a string that was stuck in the muzzle. "Please be sensible, both of you. The cork is laughable but it comes out—followed by a very real bullet."

John Henry saw his world reeling around his head. He spoke and didn't know what he said. "Mr. Jones," he croaked, "I presume?"

There wasn't a soul in the house. Thelma Loomis was ready to stake her professional reputation on that.

But somewhere there had to be people. The evidence of the two cars pointed that way. Of course, Lieutenant Lay might have been wrong about Robottom. Or he might have been pulling her leg. He was the kind of guy who'd think it was funny.

She opened the back door and let herself out into a little patio, where galvanized-iron trash cans and an electric garbage disposer kept silent vigil. Outdoors was brighter than ever after the inky interior of the ranch house.

Miss Loomis went around the corner and headed for the

161

higher boxlike building a hundred yards away. Suddenly, she stopped short, her hand fumbling for the snub-nosed revolver. Midway between the house and the other structure, something dark huddled on the ground, something that might have been a man. A darker blob crouched beside it.

"Good God!" she ejaculated. The second shadow had moved. Thelma Loomis was staring at the outline of a huge cat, its ears erect, its eyes gleaming brightly at her. Her hand shaking, she tried to level the muzzle of her .32 at the giant animal.

"You nearly surprised me," the cat purred. "Not quite. Nearly."

Miss Loomis took a firm grip on herself to keep from breaking and running. She forced her legs to carry her forward, up to the cat.

"Nice kitty," she said unsteadily. The cat stood up on its hind legs and stretched.

Moonlight poured over the face of Faye Jordan and the blonde woman began to understand the cat disguise. She had forgotten that she, too, was in costume. Her nerves unwound slightly and she chuckled softly.

"You're a policeman," Faye Jordan remarked.

"That's right." Thelma Loomis felt her smile slackening as she scanned the other, the unmoving shadow, with professional interest. "You certainly surprised me. Both of you."

"It's pretty fur, don't you think?" Faye said and preened the woolly material of her costume contentedly. "It zips down the back so I can get out. But I don't want to get out. I want to wear it all the time."

The other woman kneeled on the sandy ground and looked at the man huddled there. He was short and plump and dead. From the back of his neck the feather-tipped shaft of a long wooden arrow protruded. Blood had gushed forth sparingly, to dry in rivulets on his neck and his white shirt. He had been dead for some time, she decided.

"Who's this?" she asked.

"Oh, I don't know," Faye rubbed the back of one black mitten under her round chin. "I don't think we've ever met." "Who killed him?"

"I did," the girl said carelessly, her round eyes shiny. Thelma Loomis got up slowly, the revolver ready. "I have claws. Not everyone has claws as sharp as mine." The girl crooked her mittened hands and scratched languorously in the air.

The blonde inspected the too-bright eyes, the vacuous pretty face with its tip-tilted nose and jaw now slack. "Why?" she asked softly.

Faye Jordan looked reproachful. "I hope you're not going to ask all those questions, too."

"Who else asked you questions?"

The girl assumed a mysterious expression and prowled away toward the stable. Thelma Loomis followed her into the shadows, her gun butt damp in her hand.

Faye was swinging gaily on the wooden gate to one of the stalls. It creaked rustily back and forth like a badly tuned violin.

Miss Loomis lanced the gloom with her flashlight. The bright beam wavered. On the straw of the stall lay another form, a loose white sack of a man with arms and legs limply extended. The dark hawk face was relaxed and babyish. The man's head was lopsided with swelling under one half of the mussed silver hair. By Sagmon Robottom's ear rested a discarded stirrup iron.

Faye's gate swung in slow tortured rhythm.

"What happened here?" the blonde woman asked gently. Robottom's chest rose and sank regularly and an eyelid twitched.

"He didn't believe I was a cat." Faye crouched on the stable floor and the creaking came to a halt. Her mouth contracted viciously but the rest of her face was puzzled. "I think he said I mustn't use my claws. I don't like people who order me around."

163

"Would you like to go for a ride?" Thelma Loomis suggested soothingly. "Just the three of us. I know somebody you'd like to talk to, Faye. A man."

"Oh, that's a good idea." Faye bobbed her head excitedly. "I like to talk to men!"

Mr. Trim howled with laughter. His mouthful of irregular teeth was a wide circle and his shoulders shook. But the sound was thin, not carrying far enough to spawn an echo from the rock walls. Though his merriment was deep, neither his damp brown eyes nor the corked tip of his disguised pistol wavered away from the Conovers.

He stopped suddenly. "Shock can certainly produce a variety of comical expressions," Trim said with a final chuckle. "And yours rank with the finest in my collection. First, however—" his voice turned sharper "—gently toss that .45 back to me, Conover."

John Henry made his paralyzed hand reach for it.

"Gently. Not that I trusted you with a loaded gun—but, on the other hand, you might now be tempted to club me with it."

Carefully, John Henry lobbed the automatic to the other man. Trim snatched it deftly from the air and put it in his belt. Without shifting his gaze, he pounded his wooden pistol down sharply on the saddle horn. The painted toy shell shattered. He peeled the broken pieces from around a short black revolver and flung them to the canyon floor. "No need for masquerade any longer, is there?" he commented. The trigger of the revolver had been the only portion protruding from its gaudy camouflage.

Sin finally found a tremulous portion of her voice. "Then you're not really a G-man, at all?"

Trim smiled sparingly and shook his head. "Let's say that I'm really—" he touched the cocked hat "—a pirate. That's closer to the truth than my other personalities."

164

The moon slipped past the jagged edge of the canyon above them and the little man became a malevolent shadow against the gray gloom of wind-carved stone.

"Just one thing I want to know," said John Henry. He sagged wearily in his saddle. "Then I'll shut up. Where did you have that combination? We searched you."

"Not very thoroughly," said the shadow. "You missed the pistol, for one thing. But the combination wasn't there. The combination was here."

"Where's he pointing?" asked John Henry, straining forward.

"His mouth!" cried Sin.

"That's right," chuckled Trim. "My dentures are false. No one thinks of that. Whoever heard of owning a set of false teeth that look worse than real ones? No self-respecting dentist would make them. Everybody assumes that they must be natural—but they're as false as that story about Mr. Robottom, which I consider pretty adequate for the spur of the moment." He peered to see the extent of the Conovers' chagrin and drew back satisfied. "Enjoy the sweep of the joke," he commanded. "Others among my foes have been fooled and appreciated it."

"Mr. Trim," said John Henry earnestly. "We are not your foes. From the beginning, we've only—whoa, Nightmare!" The horse wanted to carry him forward but Conover felt he was close enough to the other man.

"No," said Sin.

"Nonsense. You've been a complication since Saturday night—although a curious one. It was an accident that Barselou learned we were in the game at all. But then to have you gullible innocents mistaken for us—I call that highly amusing. Wouldn't you?"

"No," said Sin.

"We? Us?" questioned John Henry tentatively.

"My daughter Faye and I," replied Trim blandly. "My

165

name is Jordan—if names mean anything. But don't break the habit of a week end, I beg you."

"Oh!" gasped Sin. "Then she—then we—"

"Haven't you noticed the family resemblance—the Jordan nose? It's turned up at the world—pushed into that position by generations of well-applied thumbs. Yes, it was Faye who insisted the cottages be switched so she could go through your belongings for this precious combination while they were being moved. Gayner, poor fumbler, didn't suspect a thing—he was that eager to search your stuff himself. But he searched the clothes after Faye had finished and it was he who mussed them so deplorably. And spilled your peppermint, Mrs. Conover."

Sin trembled with rage. "You killed him! And you can remember that silly peppermint in the same breath!"

"Relax, honey," said John Henry uneasily.

"Yes," chortled their captor, "you might frighten Barselou. Though he's probably so busy chopping into chests of pearls and emeralds that he couldn't hear Judgment Day. I hope he's saving me the trouble of the heavy work."

John Henry sensed that his wife was shivering, although the dark of the new day was not chilly between the protective canyon walls. He edged his horse closer to hers so that their legs touched comfortingly. "Let's move on," said John Henry and his voice was tired. "Let's get it all over with."

There was enough light for him to see Trim raise the short fat revolver menacingly. "No rush," was the amiable reply. "I prefer to board the Queen by daylight. Barselou is an excellent shot." He settled back on his steed luxuriously. His proud voice said, "Faye's taking you to the Bar C in the first place was impromptu, Conover—but it shows her flair. That way she was able to separate you from your wife and go through the only clothes of yours she hadn't inspected—the clothes you were wearing the night before."

"Then it was Faye, after all. I thought Barselou—"

"Barselou wasn't even aware that you were at his ranch at

166

all. Oh, Barselou is unaware of many things." The chuckle out of the darkness was malignant.

"And I let you rescue me from Vernon and Gayner!" cried Sin in disgust.

"Merely protecting my investment," Trim assured her smoothly.

"Just how," asked John Henry, "did you know Anglin had wandered into our cottage in the first place? If you were watching, why didn't you catch him outside?"

"Careless Anglin," clucked the man with the gun commiseratingly, "baffled by so little. Faye was waiting for him in the cottage next to yours. When she saw you turn on all your cottage lights, curiosity got the better of her. She crept over and—behold!—Anglin had left his signature by your front door. A handprint in blood. She immediately phoned me in the bar. By a stroke of fortune I was chatting with that voluble Loomis woman who told me all about your quiz contest. My mind leaped instantaneously to the obvious— I would gain entrée to your company by being the Bry-Ter Tooth-Paste man. If you had checked closely, you'd have found that Bry-Ter pays its bills from Los Angeles and does not provide a St. Christopher for its travelers."

Sin shook her red hair unbelievingly. "You must be insane!" she whispered. Then the rashness and the truth of what she had said caught in her throat.

The little figure under the pirate hat stiffened and John Henry felt his flesh prickle coldly. "No," said Mr. Trim softly. "Merely irreverent."

In a gayer voice he said, "Faye is adept. She went to the Bar C Ranch tonight to discover the starting point for the route I gained from Gayner. It was no error—her releasing you two. We didn't suspect you knew Walking Skull was the point and we were through with you. But what I commend her for is the way she waited, lurking in the shadows, guessing I would come along eventually and need her."

"No!" said Sin. "She couldn't have—" A vagrant memory

167

chilled her mind. Just the night before, when they were only on the edge of this whirlpool, she had sighed lightly to her husband, "That Jordan girl's crazy."

"Yes—my daughter. She removed Odell at the proper moment."

"She couldn't!" said John Henry, almost angrily. "I tried that longbow—she isn't strong enough!"

"Does an arrow necessarily connote a bow behind it? Odell was stabbed with the arrow—not shot with it."

Sin put her hand over her mouth to hold back the unbelieving sobs that wanted to come.

"Don't, honey," said her husband. "It doesn't help anything."

"No, nothing can be changed for most people," Trim said briskly. "Only for an aggressive handful." He peered up at the jagged streak of sky. It was lightening, with faint points of gray and pink. "Forward march!" he commanded cheerfully. "But this time we'll reverse the order. You, Conover, will go first—and I will bring up the rear. After you, please." He reined the bay horse aside to allow John Henry to pass. "I am counting on you, Conover. I count on you to realize that your first foolish move will send a bullet through your wife's spine."

"I get you," John Henry said and the sickly hope of a galloping escape among the twisting canyons died within him.

"Left here," Trim murmured.

The smoke was strong now. The horses lifted their heads. From near at hand sounded a soft whinny.

"Right at the next one," the wizened pirate ordered.

They were shields for him, Sin realized. If Barselou were at the galleon and aroused, his first shots would find helpless targets. She prayed impotently that some providence would intervene.

They clip-clopped around the last corner. A few yards away, a brush fire had been built in the lee of a great boulder. The smoke eddied up lazily over the rock and drifted in

168

a lazy thread down the canyon toward them. Two horses stood near the rock, their forelegs hobbled. The roan threw up his head and whinnied again softly in greeting.

The trio rode slowly forward, the only sounds the crackle of brush and the ring of hoofs. This final canyon had a wide sandy floor. Trim held his short revolver poised, eyes snapping from cliff to cliff. He spurred forward as they came abreast of the mammoth boulder. Then he reined his horse up and leaned both arms on the saddle horn, the gun dangling casually from one clawlike hand. His thin-lipped smile was triumphant.

A man lay beside the fire, his big body swathed in a blanket. The regular rise and fall of a bass snore betrayed the depth of his sleep.

"There is Mr. Barselou," Trim said, his bad teeth a gleeful display. "Signed, sealed and delivered." He gestured with pistol, up the canyon, toward the shadows. "And there is the Queen."

CHAPTER FOURTEEN

A<small>T FIRST</small>, Sin couldn't see it. Then, as she lifted a hand to shield her eyes from the bright embers of the campfire, she could discern a shadow darker than the rest. "Is that it, Johnny?"

"Don't ask me," John Henry muttered. "I can't see a thing."

Mr. Trim held his eyes on the sleeping Barselou but motioned with his head. "Look up, Conover. It's in the sky. Another *Flying Dutchman*."

John Henry followed his advice. The jigsaw line of sky seemed to brighten with sudden effort and the outline of a wooden hull slowly took form against the rosy glow. The *Reina* had not come to rest on the canyon bottom. Rather, the galleon was wedged between the rock jaws of the chasm, almost two hundred feet above their heads. Either the ground had eroded beneath her keel in the past two centuries or some convulsion of the wasteland had dropped her below ground level into the great gap. The Queen was earthbound, as in some gigantic dry dock. Her timber sides gripped the sister cliffs, but her round belly scorned the earth and rested on air alone.

The dawn clicked to a shade of yellow and the aloof Queen seemed to pose in the fresh light.

Awestruck, Sin murmured, "Poor lonely thing. There's not much left of her."

She was right. The sails and masts and most of the high stern had rotted away, exposing three layers of deck to their gaze. Below the galleon, near Barselou's temporary camp, was a pile of rubble that had fallen over the years. The heap was overgrown by the octopus vines of a green succulent,

170

but here trailed a rusty length of chain and there jutted a crumbling plank from the rudder.

"There's enough to prove she used to be a treasure ship, anyway," Trim's jubilant voice cried.

His gaze sharpened. The sleeping form on the ground stirred, moaned and raised itself on its elbows. "Good morning, Mr. Barselou!" Trim greeted him. His voice was climbing back to the octave the Conovers were more familiar with.

Barselou scrambled to his feet, still half-fettered by the heavy blanket. His jet-black hair stood in tangled spikes and his pale eyes were heavy with sleep. He wore whipcord breeches and a heavy brown shirt. His boots had not been removed for his rest, but the tops were partially unlaced.

His eyes widened, then narrowed at the three mounted figures above him in the dawn. One hairy hand twitched toward the carbine that lay on the ground and Trim said, "No." Barselou halted, warily motionless, and looked at the pistol muzzle while the blanket slipped to a crumpled mass about his feet.

"Rude to awaken you like this," Trim pattered on. "Particularly to the noise of a dream castle crumbling about your ears. But that's the picaresque life, isn't it?"

Barselou shifted his colorless gaze to the Conovers and his shoulders hunched grimly. "Odell," he gritted in a voice charged with venom.

"You won't have to worry about Mr. Odell," Trim said. "Mr. Anglin, Mr. Odell, Mr. Gayner—all gone. And that young bellhop is being closely questioned by the police. Calamity has come."

Barselou sagged visibly. His rugged face turned gray and he leaned for support against the boulder beside him. His colorless eyes, which seemed suddenly deeper in their sockets, glinted weakly at the Conovers. "It was you—" he began hoarsely, then stopped as if the effort were too much.

"No," said Sin earnestly. "We're here by accident. Don't you understand? *He's* Jones."

171

"Or Trim. Or Jordan," said the little man gaily. "Yes, don't give these two credit for my adventuring. The Conovers were brought because they knew of Walking Skull and for company through the night. And principally—" his voice gained metallic edges "—because they stumbled onto one of my last resorts in my wallet. Something I didn't care to have publicized. I suppose a lot of their knowledge is dangerous."

"Jones," said Barselou dully.

"A mailing address only." Trim chuckled merrily. "It's comical that you took it for more than that. At this point, there's no harm in telling you that my real name is Jordan, widower, age fifty-five, one daughter, and racing interests on the coast which return me enough to indulge my hobby of seeking out the exotic in life. We're both members of the sporting world, Mr. Barselou, though we've never met. Quite a while ago I owned a couple of casinos in Las Vegas. Homer Anglin once worked for me.

"Anglin," he mused and shook his head. "A borderline case of ingenuity. He remembered my penchant for the odd and hurried to me with news of the Queen which you hired him to discover. I knew he was selling to both sides, but he thought he held the reins secretly. His blunder was to disregard my instructions to communicate by mail when all was ready. He was in such a big hurry that he telegraphed."

Barselou lifted his head. "I was pressing him." Color began pouring back into the fierce face. "So you guessed I saw the wire."

"I couldn't ignore the chance, considering the hold you had in Azure. I generally include a female companion in my exploits—they kick up such a blinding dust. And in this case it was a sort of celebration. My daughter Faye had just been released from—" Trim halted abruptly to glare at the pale couple on the horses beside him. "She was held illegally. Her only illness was over-originality!

"Forget that carbine!" he snapped, twisting back toward

172

Barselou. The unmounted man shrugged and dropped his hands. Trim continued pleasantly. "So we had to separate for the time being, as you were expecting a pair of Joneses. The cottage had been reserved for a week, but with no mention of number or sex. All arrangements had been made for an appointment with Anglin there—except the day. When he wired instead of writing, Faye was forced to occupy the cottage alone, while I took a room. We didn't dare to bear the least resemblance to a Mr. and Mrs. Jones of San Diego. To make a quick story of it, Anglin made a stupid mistake over the cottage number, thought I had reneged on the deal, and turned to you in desperation. I couldn't catch him, but I stopped him."

Barselou rubbed his palm under his rough chin. "And I blamed Odell—"

Sin and John Henry sat silently, detached. They were watching a play on which the curtain would fall soon and they could applaud this magnificent little performer who smiled and nodded birdlike while he explained the murders of three men. But now Trim glanced overhead quickly. There was a tinge of gold on the cliff edges that reared ten feet or so above the imprisoned galleon.

"Light enough to work by," he said happily. "I presume that's what you slept away these precious hours for, Mr. Barselou. Well, shall we join the lady?"

Lieutenant Lay tossed the statement on his desk and said, "Run through it again."

Sagmon Robottom pulled his swollen head up from his hands. His sun-browned skin was mottled with pallor and the crop of silver hair still stood up haphazardly. He sat on a hard wooden chair beside Lay's desk in the cubbyhole that served the homicide chief as an office.

"I did the wrong thing," he said hoarsely. All the hard planes of his face were broken. Lines that had been stern now seemed confused and ineffectual.

173

"I got that right here." Lay tapped the statement. "Run through those bare facts again." Leaning against the closed door, Thelma Loomis brushed ashes from her blue patrolman uniform.

Robottom cleared his throat. "I'm an archaeologist, Lieutenant. I first told the story of the lost Spanish galleon to Barselou more than a year ago. Naturally, I was eager to locate it. So was he and—well, we pooled our talents."

"Sounds like a queer combination to me."

"As time passed, I discovered that Barselou regarded the ship almost fanatically. I knew that it was the *Reina's* jewels rather than the relics. I made myself overlook his personal motives. But believe me, Lieutenant, I didn't realize how far he'd go!" His colorless voice pleaded as best it could.

"Go on," said Lay inflexibly. "I don't know anything yet."

Robottom stared with gray unseeing eyes at the floor. "I supplied him with maps and what knowledge I possessed. He hired a man named Anglin to do the exploration and promised to sponsor an expedition later. A week ago I hurried here from Los Angeles. Anglin had found the ship."

"You certainly hurried," Thelma Loomis put in.

Robottom looked momentarily surprised and then went on, "Barselou phoned me Saturday night that the expedition was upset. A man and a woman named Jones, masquerading under the name of Conover, were trying to beat us to the *Reina*." Robottom squirmed on the hard seat. "Lieutenant, those relics would have doubled my reputation. I had to discover them first!"

"All right."

"I thought I might be able to bluff the Conovers out. I talked to the woman and thought I had succeeded. I was wrong. I found that out when they killed Gayner and made their getaway. By this time, I was very frightened. I hadn't bargained for murder."

"So you went out to the Bar C to talk things over with Barselou," Lay prompted.

174

"I've told everything." Robottom's face flushed slightly. "I was looking for him in the ranch house when I heard horses gallop away toward the south. When I went out to the stable, I discovered that Odell too had been murdered—but apparently by the Jordan girl. I tried to remonstrate with her and—well—"

"You got slugged," Miss Loomis said, enjoyably.

"—and your policewoman rescued me."

The homicide chief glanced her way and passed it off with a "Sure."

"What about this Faye Jordan, anyway?" Lay pressed. "I understand you know her pretty well, Robottom." The blonde woman cocked her head.

"I met her once—this morning. That's all, Lieutenant. We talked for a few minutes and I gave her a card to Barselou's —ah—"

"Casino," said Lay evenly. "I know about it." He consulted Thelma Loomis' skeptical expression and then turned again to the man across the desk. "You might be in pretty hot water now, you know that? Conspiracy, possible accessory to a murder, intimidation—"

Robottom attempted to straighten the creases of his soiled white trousers but his strong hands were shaking. He raised his tired face finally. "What are you going to do to me, Lieutenant?"

"What'll you do if I let you go?"

No hopeful shade crept into Robottom's eyes. His dull voice replied automatically. "Why—I'll go home—my wife—"

Lay nodded and made a gesture of dismissal. "Lieutenant— do you—"

The police officer said, "Recognizance and this statement will do me for the time being. Just keep in touch."

Sagmon Robottom stood up abruptly and the wooden chair clattered against the confining wall. Thelma Loomis moved away from the door.

The archaeologist looked from one to the other, tried to

175

say something and then went out abruptly. The sound of his footsteps along the corridor died away.

"Poppycock," the woman said at last.

"Don't you think he'll run all the way home to Myra?"

"Sure—right now. He's had the scare of his life. But it won't last."

"You ought to read valentines instead of divorce rates," Lay said mockingly. "If we'd told him who you are, he wouldn't have even had Myra." Fingers of sunrise were reaching across his desk. He got up and squeezed around it.

"Damn mess!" he said with sudden harshness. "I got a hunch the worst part isn't over."

"What about the girl?" Thelma Loomis asked curiously.

"We agree she's nuts. I'll check the asylums. I don't think she just cracked—she's been cracked before. Maybe there's relatives." He plucked his hat off a battered filing cabinet. "I can't make answers out of her cat talk but at least she definitely places the Conovers at the ranch last night."

Thelma Loomis opened the door and they stepped out into the cool dimness. At the end of the corridor, the dawn was a pale glow. "So the next step is to find the Conovers," Lay said softly. "They think they're sitting pretty. Well, they don't know it, but they're in a tight spot."

It took them a half hour to climb the two hundred feet up to the suspended ship. Anglin had done his work well. A rough ladder of deep steps had been chipped in the soft stone of one cliff, leading up to the stern of the Queen.

John Henry, Barselou, Sin, Trim with his revolver—that was the order. Sin had never been so frightened in her life. The armed maniac was terrifying but unreal. There was no denying the actuality of being twenty-five, then fifty, then a hundred feet in the air with a gun at her heels and the hard ground a grim distance below. Sin clutched at the crude stone steps and kept her eyes as nearly closed as she dared. Then suddenly, to one side, was a rotting balcony of sand-

176

covered wood. She grabbed for it and John Henry pulled her onto the deck of the galleon.

They huddled in the exact center of the platform, neither caring to look down the way they'd come.

"No wonder I couldn't spot it from the air," Barselou muttered. This topmost deck was heaped with sandy dirt and small rocks. Sagebrush, mesquite, a few struggling wild flowers had taken root. From above, it would seem a piece with the surrounding Badlands.

The masts were three broken stumps that barely poked through the small dunes on the main deck below them. Near one rail, the pocked back of a cannon still showed above the sand. John Henry looked nervously at the rock walls which held the Queen in place. Then he scanned the ground level a few feet over his head.

Trim interpreted the glance and chuckled. "No, Mr. Conover. Down into the hold. That's where the chests will be."

They were standing on the high stern deck. Barselou led the way lightly, but at every step the timbers beneath him creaked and groaned. The four picked their route gingerly across the towering deck, down a rotting flight of steps, and into the low waist of the galleon. Part of the decking had fallen away here, exposing the deck below and forming a sloping incline that joined the two levels. Barselou slid down the slope and landed with a heavy crash on the next platform. The *Reina* shuddered under the impact.

"Careful, damn you!" snapped Trim, his voice betraying the first sign of strain. "I don't want this thing to collapse while I'm here."

John Henry eased himself down the splintering boards. Then he extended a hand back to Sin. "They crossed the Pacific in this little boat?" she asked.

"They didn't know any better," said John Henry.

"The risk for the profit," Barselou said heavily. Trim was guiding himself down the incline at that moment and the big man winked significantly at John Henry. Even in this

177

weird setting, on the gun deck of a forgotten ship, he felt a rebirth of hope. After all, they were three against one—and they had nothing to lose.

Trim sidled away from them, his pug-nosed face leaning over the pistol barrel as though he had scented their thoughts. "I warn you. I shed my compunctions easily." The skull and crossbones cockade on his hat didn't seem ridiculous here.

Sin shuddered up against her husband. She nudged him and extended a trembling forefinger. "Look at them!" Sprawled around the deck in haphazard piles were collections of bleached bones. A skull stared at them with hollow eyes as the rising sun caressed it.

"Some of Arvaez' crew," Barselou said, and his tones were almost scholarly.

A cannon lay helplessly on one side by a roughly square hole that had once been a hatch. Sin held tightly onto John Henry's hand and peered around at the dimlit recess beneath and at the dusty timbers that curved up to meet the flooring they stood on. Two of the great planks had sprung and almost directly beneath her she could see the five horses in the canyon, two hundred feet below. She drew back shivering.

Trim, in his red knee breeches and long blue coat, seemed a fit commander for the ghost ship. He wasn't looking at the bones on the cannon or the empty hold. His sharp eyes raced around the corners of the shadowy deck. Then he let out a whoop of triumph.

Against a moldering bulkhead, far forward, was a row of squat chests. "There!" he ordered. "Hurry—open them up!" The four people moved cautiously toward the ironbound boxes. Barselou and John Henry wrestled with the first chest of the row, prying at the lid. It creaked and gave a little, sifting rust onto the timbers.

"Together," grunted Barselou. The two men panted in unison and forced it open. They stared into the black depths.

178

John Henry lifted his head first and looked at the man in the pirate costume.

"False alarm," he said. "It's empty."

"Don't lie!" Trim rasped.

"Why should I? It's empty. There's nothing in it."

Trim bounded forward and drove the other two aside with the gun. A moment later, he raised a face that was pale and contorted with rage. Barselou still gazed at the opened chest as if hypnotized. His countenance had gone dead.

"Get back!" Trim commanded, panic in his words. His lower jaw hung open as if he had forgotten about it and his wet tongue moved back and forth over his ugly teeth. Sin and the two men backed up. Their captor's brown eyes flicked between them and the treasure chests as he went down the row kicking at the dusty ironbound tops. Most of the lids flew back instantly, banging against the bulkhead. A red dust arose and sunbeams danced on flakes of rust.

At the last chest, Trim uttered a howl and dipped his free hand deep within it. He pulled out a fistful of round black objects like withered marbles and held them close to his face, staring uncomprehendingly. Then he pivoted and hurled the tiny wrinkled balls spitefully at Barselou.

"There's your fabulous riches!" he shrieked. "There's the Queen's jewels!" He capered around madly, his joints jerking as though marionette strings guided him. His high cracked voice screamed curses at Barselou until gasps of spent breath stopped the obscene flow.

The withered black globules lay patternless on the sandy timbers. Sin gazed at them and remembered something she'd read. Pearls, exposed to the elements over a long period of time, deteriorate and become valueless.

"I don't understand," Barselou said dully. "I don't understand."

"Maybe you can understand this," Trim panted, waving his arms. "Somebody beat you to the gold, the emeralds, all

179

the treasure. Somebody maybe a century ago. Can you get that through your thick head? Somebody else found the galleon first! Anglin knew! Anglin was double-crossing us both!"

John Henry laughed. He couldn't help it, he couldn't restrain it even in the face of maniacal fury. Barselou's search, Trim's involved intrigue—all had been for nothing. Three men had died for a chest of worthless pearls. Anglin had known and he had profited most from the Queen. But Anglin hadn't been clever enough.

Sin laughed too. She crossed her arms in front and tried to hold back the mirth. "It's another Spoonerism," she giggled, caught up in the frenzy that charged the air.

"What?" said John Henry.

"Spooner," she repeated, her shoulders shaking. "You know—the man who always got his words twisted."

"What about him?"

Sin giggled harder than ever. Her words trailed up hysterically. "Remember? Somebody asked him if he sang and Mr. Spooner said, 'I know only two tunes—God Save the Weasel and Pop Goes the Queen.' Don't you get it, Johnny? She just popped!"

And Sin went off into gales of laughter.

"Stop it! Stop it!" yelled Trim. He thrust the muzzle of his revolver almost in Sin's face. Her peal of laughter became a tangled sob. "Get over against the wall—all of you!" commanded the little man. Flecks of light were dancing oddly in his eyes. He hissed softly, "This is high tragedy. I will not accept the role of clown. I will not accept it."

Sin and John Henry backed up silently, Barselou mechanically.

"There. Right there," barked Trim as three backs touched the side of the galleon. The trio stood on a wide curb of wood that surrounded the entire deck—the gun platform. Behind them, the rectangular cannon ports revealed the rock face of the cliff, blind and gray.

180

Something hard bobbed against Sin's neck and she ducked. From a beam that ran the length of the ship's side, several rusty iron chains dangled. Each chain terminated in a wide iron cuff. The ship's irons, designed for lazy or mutinous seamen of His Majesty's Navy.

Trim was addressing Barselou. "Snap those chains around their wrists, if you please."

John Henry looked around desperately. Sin licked her trembling lips and asked, "What are you going to do, Mr. Trim? Please—"

"An old pirate custom, Mrs. Conover." A wrinkled hand pulled the cocked hat lower over spangled flickering eyes. "No prisoners. By the time you're found, you'll be indistinguishable from the other skeletons here."

"No—you can't—" Sin choked. She almost fell to her knees but John Henry held her to him.

The threatening pistol motioned at Barselou. The big man reached for the dangling chains. The muscles in his face were working now, but his eyeballs were transparent, far away, as though he were pondering some weighty problem. Barselou's grasping mind had been numbed by the loss of the treasure.

"Johnny—don't let him—"

Conover struggled but the expressionless gambler was inexorable. Machine-like, Barselou forced John Henry's wrists into the iron circlets. It needed all the power in his hairy hands to press the rusty gyves together.

Sin submitted limply. The pair stood side by side on the gun platform, their wrists held at ear level by the ancient cuffs anchored to chains from the beam above.

Barselou wheeled slowly and said, "What next?" He looked at the man with the gun disinterestedly.

Trim smiled but his mouth was stiff and his instructions panted through it. "It's your turn, Mr. Barselou. Face the wall."

Dumbly, the big man obeyed.

"Put your hands up just like the others." Trim stepped catlike across the deck and shoved the mouth of his pistol into the small of Barselou's back. "Now just hold still."

John Henry felt the perspiration beading his palms. He held his breath back and waited for the moment, the only possible moment. A muscle twitched where Barselou's shirt was tight across his huge shoulders.

John Henry lashed out with his foot at Trim's kneecap. The little man danced back, howling, and stumbled on the uneven timbers. Sin screamed.

Over her treble shriek came the blanketing roar of colossal rage. With one motion, Barselou jerked a rusty chain loose from its mooring and whipped it ferociously at the cocked hat. The hat spun away crazily. Trim sank to one knee in the center of the gun deck, blood streaming from his bald head. He raised the revolver.

John Henry fought to escape the gyves. He got one hand free of the loose cuff of iron. But Barselou had leaped. With another reverberating roar, he sprang from the gun platform for the crouched figure. The pistol exploded against his chest and in the narrow bowels of the galleon it was like a cannon blast.

Barselou's huge body enveloped the little man, his knees and fists battering, pummeling, mauling. Trim howled and his revolver blasted again.

The deafening noise joined the echoes of the first explosion. They bounded against rocky walls up and down the canyon, doubling and redoubling, until the wooden ship was a trembling fury.

The *Reina* groaned, shuddered. Then she began to move.

"—collapsing!" Trim yelled in a piercing voice and tried to claw his way from beneath Barselou's flailing bulk. John Henry threw his free arm around Sin's waist and pulled her close.

182

A subdued rumble was born among the dying echoes. It grew louder and louder. Then the deck tilted.

Conover braced his feet as the gun platform shivered. The deck tilted more and the thrashing bodies before his hypnotized gaze rolled toward the stern. Old timbers creaked agonizingly and sand poured from above. Two of the great overhead planks parted. The stubby root of a mainmast fell through.

A convulsion seized the *Reina* as the roar of bursting seams soughed in the narrow canyon slot. Trim scrambled from Barselou's grasp and hugged the shifting deck. A hairy hand fastened around one pirate boot and pulled him back. Trim screamed.

John Henry pushed Sin's face harder against his body.

With a climactic ripping of wood, the decks of the Queen collapsed and plunged through the ancient keel for the canyon floor. Trim's final maniacal shriek spun a thread of terror as the two struggling men dropped from sight with the downpour of wreckage. The thin noise was drowned by the crash of timbers grinding into the earth below.

The sound faded away, dividing itself among other canyons until there was nothing left.

Dust swirled in the silent air.

Sin opened her eyes. Fearfully, she lifted her face from her husband's shoulder and looked around. She began to cry.

Below them yawned the emptiness of the gorge with its churning column of brown dust. They still stood on the gun platform far above the earth. The reverberations of the echoing gunshots and the violent struggles of the two men had caused most of the hull and rotten decking of the galleon to give way. But the stout curving timbers of the *Reina's* sides had remained, an empty oval between the canyon walls. The curb on which the Conovers huddled had been part of the funnel through which the ruins of the hulk

183

had poured. And the beam to which three of their four wrists were gyved had stayed up as part of the plank spider web holding the hollow shell of the ship in mid-air.

"We're all right now, honey," said John Henry comfortingly. Then he found his voice and repeated it out loud. Sin kept on sobbing. "It's okay, Sin."

"I know, Johnny," she whimpered. "That's why I'm crying."

Gingerly, Conover pried at their iron cuffs. Two of the rusty hinges bent open easily. His own gyve broke apart in his hands. He tossed the pieces at the wreckage below.

The dust cloud was thinning and settling now. He could make out the dead campfire and the startled horses neighing and rearing at the new mountain of rubble that had poured from the sky. To the east, the red disk of morning sun had just topped the mountains to beam on the jigsaw cracks of the Badlands.

John Henry took a deep breath. As soon as Sin felt better, they'd climb down the cliff again to the horses. In the daylight, it would be easy to retrace their trail to Walking Skull —and then civilization. It was going to be another hot day.

Sin finally got her sobs under control. They looked down into the depths of the canyon silently. Far below, nothing moved in the heap of broken timbers that had once been the Manila galleon.

"Funny," she said softly. "I feel sorrier for the Queen than I do for anybody."

Her husband put a gentle arm around her waist. To one side of the wreckage, John Henry thought he saw the crushed shape of a three-cornered hat.

"The poor old Queen," he agreed. "It took a long time for the pirates to catch her. But, Sin, she put up a wonderful fight."

184